THE MALEDICTION PLAGUE

THE MALEDICTION PLAGUE

SIRRAH MEDEIROS

Tundra Swan Press

Virginia

Editor: Genie Rayner, Magic Lamp Editing Services
Cover Design: Sirrah Medeiros, Tundra Swan Press
Cover Images: Molecule image from Science Photo Library, Canva Pro Content license. Bloody Hand image by Shalunx13 from Getty Images and Canva Pro Content license.

Paperback ISBN: 979-8-9852025-4-0
eBook ISBN: 979-8-9852025-5-7

Library of Congress Control Number: 2024905517

Published by Tundra Swan Press LLC
TundraSwanPress.com

CONTENT WARNING

This story touches on abuse, psychological trauma, main character racial views, as well as graphic depictions of gore.

The scariest monsters are the ones that lurk within our souls.

—Edgar Allan Poe

PREFACE

"You can't be serious?" Zoey asked as she dropped her hand to the table. Her glass slipped from her fingertips and red wine sloshed onto the crisp white linen.

Leon gave a huff. "That's going to set." Mortified by the crimson stain, he quickly blotted at the spot with his napkin, then threw it down. He left and came back with a roll of paper towels and peeled off several sheets, then jabbed at the mess.

Leon walked out of the room again, leaving Zoey to stare after him, stunned.

Leon snorted as he strode back in and stopped next to the table with an industrial-sized bottle of hydrogen peroxide and other cleaning supplies.

Zoey shook her head and went into the kitchen as Leon made his mixture and poured it over the stain. She washed her hands, wiped them dry, and then neatly folded the towel, placing it back on the rack exactly as she'd found it. How Leon had showed her several times in the past, before she started positioning it as she'd found it, so he wouldn't follow her and rearrange its placement. He'd do so with everything anyone touched in his apartment. Zoey remembered how it annoyed her the first time he did it and he had told her how he liked this or that placed just so in his house.

She crunched up her face at the memory.

Zoey didn't venture back to the dining table, but stared at her fiancé as he fixated on the task of removing the spilled wine.

Her face reddened.

"Are you done?"

Silence.

Annoyed by his lack of response, Zoey continued. "What do you mean, you literally hate children? That's ridiculous."

Leon blotted and sprayed, analyzed the spot, then repeated his actions without looking up. "You've heard me say 'I hate children' numerous times. This isn't news, Zoe."

"Yes, but everyone says that around bratty kids. They don't mean it for *all* children."

"Well, I do," Leon said flatly.

Zoey thought about her childhood, growing up with her little sister, Ella. The two girls were close from the moment Ella learned to walk and followed Zoey everywhere ... until they pursued education at different colleges. Zoey was fascinated with living things and studied biology. Ella loved flowers, but her academic interests pulled her toward a computer career in cyber security. The sisters remained close.

Ella was younger but already had two children. A little jealous of Ella's family life, Zoey had hoped she would soon have a child, too. Perhaps two or three, so her children would bond with their cousins as well as she and Ella had over the years. She wanted to teach her children about gardening and living off the land. How to grow plants and herbs just as her mother and grandmother had taught her and Ella.

Turning her attention back to Leon, she saw a future without children. Anger flared now at herself. How could she have been so blind? She never asked the tough questions like politics, or religion, or if he wanted a family. Instead, she ignored the tiny warnings her intuition raised from time to time. The little flairs in her mind that said, "He isn't for you."

Now she was engaged. But seeing Leon tonight, clearly for the first time, she had to make a change for herself. Zoey had wasted two years of her life with him. No more.

She slid the engagement ring off her finger and tossed it on the counter.

The tinny clank of metal on granite amplified in their silence.

Leon lifted his head.

Zoey took a breath and let it out slowly. "Leon, it's over."

That's when the argument began.

CHAPTER ONE

THE LAB

"It's about damn time." Dr. Leon Fleischer bent over the microscope, taking note of his findings. Fueled with nervous energy, he watched as the serum flowed toward one cell, punctured the membrane, and conjoined with the host. The serum was at last complete, ready for animal trials. If they could get past the trials, then transferring the serum to capsule form would follow.

He leaned back in his chair and ran his hands through his rumpled hair as he looked around the laboratory. He had spent day and night within these sterile walls the past few weeks. No others kept him company. His surroundings were more sanitary than a hospital, the lingering smell of disinfectant in the air, but he no longer noticed. The white ceilings, walls, even the white floors were a stark contrast to the black metal pens. His only company were the caged rats and mice lining the length of one wall and stacked several cages high. The confined creatures scurried quietly as Leon ranted aloud about his circumstances. Throughout the two months since Zoey suddenly broke off their engagement, the solitary answers he received were the soft rustling of tiny nails scampering along sawdust-covered flooring.

Her actions continued to perplex him. *What went wrong?* His head shook as he thought back to their dinner date and the last conversation. She'd dropped her ring on the kitchen counter and walked out. He followed her out the door and down the hall to the elevator holding the engagement ring in his fingertips. They yelled and argued over each other until she shoved him out of the way and the elevator doors closed in his face.

After he'd left several messages the following day, she returned his call.

"Leon, it's over between us. I can't support the work that you do any more than you can change the way I feel about having children. I want a family and it's plain by your beliefs about the world, overpopulation, and even abortion that you will never want children. Consider your profession. Nothing I say or do will change your views on the matter. I thought you would change your mind when we talked about getting married, but I was obviously very wrong," Zoey seethed through the receiver. Her voice grew louder and the pitch higher as she spoke.

Leon pulled the phone from his ear, bewildered. He raised a brow and shook his head before giving a reply.

"Zoey, why bring this up now? You knew what you were getting into when we started dating. I was upfront about my research, my thoughts on the state of the world. The work I do at Aionios Pharmaceuticals is something I truly love. I know you didn't agree with it, but my work didn't appear to be a deal breaker for you. You never mentioned wanting to have children. Why do you have this sudden rash of judgment and change of heart toward us?"

"Things change, Leon."

"I understand that, but what things? What has changed so drastically that you feel the need to end our engagement now? That is what I don't understand."

"And I can't explain it to you, Leon. It's simply different … everything is different. It's clear that we will never agree on these matters. I realized I can't live like that. I can't build a future with you."

Then she hung up on him.

He sat in his small apartment, the handset to the rotary phone his parents had in their home when he was growing up dangled from his fingertips. Nostalgic for the past, he gawked at it, unable to comprehend that Zoey not only broke off their engagement for reasons he didn't understand, but that she had no intention to continue their relationship on any level.

Two months had gone by since they last spoke. Repeatedly he tried to talk with her, calling or stopping by her apartment. She wouldn't answer him. He was left to do the only thing he knew to do. He poured himself into his work, pushing everything else, including thoughts of Zoey, out of his mind. With nothing pulling him from his research, Leon worked at the lab, day and night, on the new serum. He'd inherited the project from his predecessor. The poor man died of a heart attack, leaving Leon eager to assume control.

He was far ahead of schedule. The extra time he'd put into the project finally paid off. Exhausted, bitter, and in tatters from working with little sleep, he pushed himself farther on his latest project. He didn't want to go home. There was no reason to go back to an empty apartment. Consequently, he hoisted himself up from the chair to begin the next phase of research.

He took a large white mouse from the cage and felt her abdomen. He could tell she had at least two or three little ones. Employing a syringe filled with serum, he administered the needle into the abdomen, ensuring it penetrated the sac surrounding the unborn. He then placed the mouse back in the cage and waited to see the results of his endeavors.

It shouldn't take long to work. The oxytocin in the serum induces labor in the mother while the other chemicals kill what's inside, Leon thought to himself as he waited. *Too bad my grandfather didn't think of something like this during the war. He could've succeeded in his mission much more effectively without so much mess. We really would have built a supreme race, eliminating the world of vermin.*

The scowling face of his disapproving mother popped into his mind. Whenever he did something of which she disapproved, she could not hide it. Her expression always gave away what she thought. Leon shook his head as if to discard the image.

The mouse convulsed, drawing Leon out of his daydream and pulling his attention to the cage. Before squealing, the mouse thrashed for a minute as the first fetus popped out. The eyes were open and dark gray. Instead of having a pink color, the rodent's skin had an ashen tone. It was obviously void of life, no breathing or pulse.

Success. It works, he pondered while gazing at the view. Two more mice slid from the mother's underside as he watched, each one lifeless. *Finally, this is what we need, another method to reduce the world of unwanted vile children. We don't need to add to the population of a world that already overflows with humans, many of whom are not fit to produce intelligent life.*

His father and grandfather, both scientists, had Leon lost in thought, not really looking at the mice anymore, but remembering the lessons taught to him as a little boy. It was a profession passed down from generation to generation, as were the desirable physical characteristics of blond hair, fair complexion and blue eyes.

Movement caught Leon's eye. His gaze shifted downward and observed a moving fetus. Not paying attention a moment ago, he wasn't sure if it was born alive. Its color was not pink, but a lifeless gray, just like the other two. Leon peered closer. He couldn't tell if it was breathing. There was no visible movement of the chest or abdomen. Then he saw the snarled teeth as the little head raised from the cage floor, a small bit of drool hanging from a tooth. The fetus seemed to look around with smoky black, beady eyes and fix its gaze on the mother. It crawled, making a low growling noise as it moved the few inches closer to its mother. Then, wrinkling its nose as if to smell, it lashed out and tore into its mother's flesh.

Leon thrust his back into the seat cushion, almost falling off his chair.

Blood splattered across his white lab coat. Another fetus joined in the massacre, ripping the flesh from the mother just as the first had done. Leon stood up and took a few steps back as he continued to fix his gaze on the mice.

What is going on? Now all three of the newly born were climbing on the mother, tearing at her fur, ripping out muscle and tendons, feeding on her flesh.

They were not breathing. He didn't see a pulse of any kind beating through a vein, visible through the thin gray flesh. No, they did not appear to be living. Yet they were obviously alive. He took a long probe from the drawer nearby and a stethoscope, used to check their heartbeats without having to touch them or get close to where the specimens could bite the researcher. He pinned one to the corner with the probe, and then another. Nothing. No heartbeat from either was evident. Leon didn't understand.

The mother was dead now, her life eaten away by her children. Leon's curiosity grew as he watched the little creatures. The scene before him was morbid, disgusting. He should be revolted by the carnage. Yet Leon saw a miraculous event unfold due to his scientific expertise, and a surge of pride welled up from deep within him. A growing perception worked in his mind. He had done something unique in this experiment, unplanned yes, but unique. His mind churned for greater understanding of the implications of such a find as he continued to watch the tiny critters crawl to one side of the cage, clawing at the wire. A nearby enclosure filled with mice seemed to have caught their attention, and the little ones howled in protest, wanting to escape.

The mother moved, but its color drained, replaced with a gray cast. Cloudy, lifeless eyes looked around the cage. It moved to the same side of the cage where the newly born were and, using its jaws, tried to break free. Leon was stunned into silence. The mother was strong, able to move the bars with only her head and teeth.

He grabbed the cage and moved it near the incinerator. The lifeless, but not motionless, mice howled as he walked past the other cages in the lab. Stopping in his tracks, he looked at each cage and the reaction of the ones imprisoned in the enclosure he held in his hands. He slowly brought the ones he held closer to their friends in a nearby cage. The new offspring and the mother became uncontrollable, attempting to tear through the wire and reach the others. He placed the cages side-by-side so their noses could touch if they tried to reach across. The dead mother quickly gnawed through the cage and grabbed a mouse from the other cage, tearing off its nose with one bite. Swiftly removing the entire cage, Leon forcefully tossed the cage with the new mother and offspring into the incinerator. *Obviously there was something wrong in the serum, but what?* He would have to review the mixture to determine the cause of such a reaction.

As he watched the mice burn, he heard a commotion from the other cage. The newly bitten mouse was tearing at the others with what was left of its face, teeth noshing and chomping on whatever flesh the rodent could grasp in its mouth. Leon knew it no longer lived as we think of living flesh. No blood coursed through its veins, no breath filled its lungs. It was some sort of automaton, living but dead at the same time. Each victim briefly feeds on the host before transforming into a zombie and feeding on another victim.

It sickened Leon, yet at the same time fascinated him. He felt something shift in his mind. Somewhere deep within his psyche, a plan formed, a twisted, devious thought he knew would change the course of humanity. A vision his father and grandfather would be proud of, a legacy.

He took the remaining cage of mice and threw it too into the incinerator's blaze. Quickly gathering his research materials and keys, he headed home to sort through the formula and develop his new scheme.

CHAPTER TWO

FORMULA

Examining the research notes left by the initial scientist on the project, Leon was astounded he hadn't recognized the connection during the development of the abortion serum. Half of the ingredient list could be found in zombie voodoo magic used frequently in areas of the world such as Haiti and the deep south of the United States. No wonder his serum turned newborn fetuses into killing machines. Obviously there was some truth to the superstition surrounding the use of dark magic.

Tetrodotoxin, a poison found in the Japanese blowfish, Leon knew was fatal if one were to consume too much. It was used in the serum to kill the fetus, but the dosage was supposed to be low enough to prevent death in the mother. He remembered that was accurate. The mother did not die until the fetuses started feeding on her. Of course, he realized that she then turned into an undead creature herself. So there must be some sort of contagion in the serum that was transmitted once bitten by an infected specimen.

The next ingredient listed was *Datura Stramonium*, commonly known as jimson weed or devil's snare. Used in voodoo magic, a person would have hallucinations and amnesia, along with a fever. Leon wasn't sure why this was in the formula. He could only speculate that a biological benefit, combined with other ingredients, was necessary for the serum to work. He wrote a note in the lab book to look at the entire chemical composition when he was back in the research office.

Dragging his laptop over, Leon typed the ingredient name into the Google search bar and hit enter. He clicked on a title *Voodoo Potion* and started reading. Nothing new there, except the last sentence caught his attention. '... potentially strengthens the victim's belief that a real transformation took place.' Leon thought that was interesting, but it didn't add credibility to the reason it had been added to the serum. He put a question mark next to it on the ingredient list and moved on to the next one, cane toad secretions.

Bufo Marinus, also known as the cane toad, secretes a deadly toxin that Leon knew could be fatal. So strong is the toxin, small animals, such as cats and dogs, have been killed by the toad's secretions. The toxin is irritating to the skin and very painful to the eyes. Humans have died from ingesting the eggs or eating grown adult toads. If threatened, a cane toad could shoot the secretion over a meter, possibly killing or at least causing its attacker to become ill before getting close to the toad. This ability is a self-defense mechanism that helped to infiltrate the species into areas of the Southern United States where it is not native.

It did not surprise Leon this toxin was on the ingredient list. It was imperative for the abortion process and the resulting miscarriage to be complete. Since the serum was being marketed for women up to five months pregnant, it was crucial that the fetus be still born. If the fetus were born alive, then it would be considered a living person and the mother would have to care for the child. This toxin was the most important in the formula.

Leon sat back, letting his eyes rest from reading over the detailed information. There were a few other inert ingredients listed, none with significant value. He needed to sleep and get a fresh start tomorrow. A few minutes later, he was dreaming.

Leon was talking with his father and grandfather about what happened at the lab. His father was trying to convince him that Leon had discovered a new wave of technology that would allow a supreme race to rule the world. With strategic placement, the serum could wipe the lower levels of humanity from the earth, rid the world of vermin and filth, and free up needed resources for a much smaller but intelligent human society.

Leon's grandfather spoke up then. "Son, humanity needs to be reduced in numbers to save the planet from destruction. Population growth is out of control. Leon, your serum could be God's answer to humanity's selfishness. You shall work as God's disciple, brandishing the sword to the unforgivable, the forsaken, and downcast of society. Through you, God's will be done. No one unworthy will be left standing, only the chosen ones will survive. His onslaught of justice."

Drawn in by the words spoken by his father and grandfather, Leon sensed a new purpose grip his soul. He felt chosen to lead a mission of rebirth for humanity, a cleansing of the earth.

"I won't let you down. I know what I must do."

"That's my boy," Leon's father replied from far away. "Go now and start your quest. Your reward will be great. You will lead a new beginning."

The phone rang, rousing Leon from his dream. He reached over for the receiver while rubbing his eyes with his other hand.

"Hello?"

"Dr. Fleischer?"

"Yes, this is Dr. Fleischer. Who's calling?"

"Doctor, this is Chief Security Guard Mattson at the women's prison. We have a woman here who has a fever. She's about four months pregnant, sir. We can't reach the regular doc since he's on vacation. Your name is on the call roster in case of an emergency."

"Oh, yes. Yes, that is correct, Chief Mattson. I'd forgotten I was on the call roster there. What can I do for you?"

"Well, doc, like I said, this lady's got a fever, and she says she feels rough. She's only in prison for a week on some drug charge. I don't want to be blamed for her losing that baby while she's in our prison. Can you come out and look at her?"

"Yeah, sure thing. I'll be there in an hour."

"Thanks, Doc. You're a life saver."

Leon hung up the phone and sat back. His mind was still foggy from sleep so he ran the conversation with the chief in his mind again. *This woman was in prison on drug charges, sick with fever, and she's pregnant.* Something was working in his mind, but his consciousness wasn't ready to acknowledge it.

He got up slowly, went into the bathroom, and turned on the water in the shower.

CHAPTER THREE

Leon drove back to the lab to pick up his bag. He wasn't a medical doctor, so he had to gather some things from the office to treat the woman. He would need to give her some antibiotics or something to get her through until the regular doctor returned or until they transferred her to the city hospital.

In his office, he grabbed his leather bag and placed the items in it as he gathered them: a stethoscope, some general antibiotics, a blood pressure cuff, and a prescription pad. He walked past the refrigerated cabinet again and stopped before turning to look inside the clear glass door. The abortion serum was in front of him, the label clearly marked and facing him. At that moment, he remembered his dream and the words of his father and grandfather. *Was it just a dream or a sign of what he was supposed to do?*

Leon reached into the cabinet with eager glee and selected one of the opaque purple vials. Carefully, he pulled out the serum and placed it into his coat pocket. He grabbed a few syringes off the shelf and threw those into his bag. He looked around one last time, making sure he had everything he would need for the pregnant inmate, and then he left the office.

In the infirmary, Dr. Fleischer sat next to the feverish woman. The chief was right, she didn't look well. Leon asked the chief to step into the other room in case the woman was contagious. He could see Mattson was watching from the window partition with a relieved look on his face. He obviously didn't want to catch whatever sickness this woman was carrying into his prison.

Leon started with the usual tests. He took her temperature, blood pressure, and pulse. He annotated everything just as he would with any patient or lab specimen. Then, instead of giving her a dose of intravenous antibiotics, he took the syringe in his hand and filled it with the serum.

The woman shook her head and said, "No, I don't want anything to hurt my baby. Please."

Leon didn't care who she was but didn't want her to get upset either, so he asked, "What's your name? I'm Dr. Fleischer."

"Jacqueline Mitchelle, my friends call me Jackie."

"Oh, okay, Jacqueline. I'm going to take good care of you."

Leon took her arm and pulled up the sleeve. He could see the track marks from her drug use but they looked old. She must have stopped once she found out she was pregnant. Leon hesitated, wondering if the woman in front of him should be the first. He thought the phone call from the chief was a sign, delivered right after his dream. Yet his heart pounded in his chest. Wasn't he called at that precise time for a reason? His torso swelled with indignant pride, joyous for the opportunity. After all, this was a mission sent to him by God. So he took a deep breath and, while squaring his shoulders, he plunged the needle into her vein.

"It's just an antibiotic. You'll be fine and so will the fetus. Your fever is very high, and the shot will work faster than giving you pills. Don't worry, just try to get some rest and let the medicine work."

"Thank you, Doctor. I want to be a good mother, you know. Get my life together." The woman turned her head and closed her eyes.

"No problem, dear. Get some sleep. You'll feel better shortly," Leon replied as he gathered his things and placed them back in his bag.

"Chief, make sure she isn't disturbed for a few hours. You know how to reach me if there are any further concerns. Here are some antibiotics to get her through until the regular doctor is back in town. I noted everything I did on the chart next to her bed."

"Thanks, Dr. Fleischer. You've been great. No way did I want that woman to miscarry in my prison. Get her well and out the door at the end of the week. She can be some other guy's problem."

"Good plan, Chief. You say the security is tight here?" Leon asked as the chief walked him toward the prison entrance.

"Yeah. Sure, Doc. Just short of maximum security. Nothing gets in or out of here without one of us saying so. Why do you ask?"

"Oh, just curious, Chief. You have a good day."

"Thanks, Doc. You, too."

Leon climbed into his Mercedes and stared at the wall directly facing him. As Leon turned the key, he noticed his hands were shaking. *What did he just do to that woman?*

A voice in his head answered, "You're the chosen one, son. You are saving the world from trash like her."

Leon answered aloud, "I am, aren't I? I am fixing the future, making it better."

A smile played across his lips as he thought about the new world he envisioned. His mission for humanity had started tonight. Soon, he could rid the country of all the prisons. There would be no need for them when he was done.

The aversion to being home alone no longer with him, he felt reborn, new energy coursing through his veins. He was creating a new world, one rid of the filth and underachieving humans. There would be a reawakening of humanity due to his efforts, his retooling of the human race.

Happy with himself, he headed home to rest. Sleep nagged at him suddenly and he wanted to sleep in his bed.

CHAPTER FOUR

Leon realized four days had passed since he'd left the jail. He fell asleep as soon as he crawled into bed and he slept for over 24 hours, his body in desperate need of the rejuvenating effects of rest. The following days, he mulled around the apartment, read a bit of fiction, ate whatever he could find in the kitchen, drank scotch, and napped. He had no idea what was going on in the city until late afternoon on the fourth day. He finally turned on a local news channel.

The usual dress and appearance of the pretty newswoman was in shambles. Sitting up closer to the television, Leon listened to what she had to say.

"The city is still in chaos this afternoon. According to the sheriff's department, the outbreak started at the local prison and spread from there. The infected are extremely strong and do have some mental faculties remaining. Meaning they are capable of recognizing speech but have difficulty speaking themselves. They also recognize family and loved ones yet have wiped out their entire families before joining a collective group that appears to work in mass through the city. The dead go through a sort of transformation and wake in a creature-like state, an unhuman-human.

"So far, police have determined the only way to keep the creatures down, for lack of a better word, is to shoot them in the head or decapitate them. Yes, viewers, I said decapitate them.

"Do what you can to stay away from them and stay safe. The infection quickly spreads through bodily fluid contact: blood, saliva, or mucus. If you can stay indoors, please do so. If you can leave the area until the authorities deem the city safe again, that is probably the better course of action.

"What was that?"

There was a noise somewhere on the set. The news was still going live, and the newswoman was visibly terrified of what she could see but the viewers could not. Leon watched with intense interest and increased anxiety. The woman vaulted from her seat, screaming. Leon watched as three people, blood-soaked with open wounds, climbed over the desk, pinning the woman to the backdrop of the set. The camera was off-center but filming everything.

A hand flew out from the mayhem and landed on the desk. Beautifully manicured fingernails and a large sapphire ring on the index finger were visible from the bloody limb for viewers to see. Leon watched intently as the news anchor was torn apart, blood splattering across the lens as cries filled his ears. He was transfixed on the scene, studying the creatures. No breathing, skin ashy gray, eyes void of life.

Oh, but those eyes could see. The creatures on the screen were his creation, of that he was certain. He couldn't deny the characteristics of the serum he'd used just four days before. First on the mice, then on the woman in the prison. This scene, this turmoil, was not what he'd envisioned. Alarmed and confused, he stood and paced the floor. He walked past the desk several times before he noticed a light blinking on the answering machine of his landline. He stopped and pressed the button.

"Doc! Doc, what did you do to that woman?" It was Chief Mattson. "She started thrashing about shortly after you left, screaming in pain. Get over here! Doc, you there?"

The next message was from a few moments later. "Doc, what the hell? This ain't right, Doc. That baby came out dead. Dead, I tell you. I know it did. What'd you do? Get over here— we need some help! But Jackie ain't dead neither. After that ... that thing ... sprang up and clawed and gnashed at Jackie even though she was as sickly looking as the thing she cradled in her arms. They went to the infirmary, but neither one of them was dead now. They—they both came out of the infirmary as something else."

Leon heard screams beyond the chief's voice along with sounds of items being thrown around the room. "Doc, call the sheriff. We're in trouble. I can't hold 'em off by myself. Damn it, Doc. We're all doomed now. Shit!"

Leon heard the chief scream as the phone was dropped or ripped from the chief's hand. As Leon continued to listen, he heard the ruckus move throughout the building on the recording. A deep sense of dread gripped him as he realized the city's fate was due to his folly.

Yet he felt his grandfather's voice rising in his head. "Stay the course, son. This is just what the world needs to control things in the end."

Leon swung his head violently, dispelling his grandfather's voice. *Where was Zoey?*

He tried her cell phone. Nothing but a long buzz followed by a network message that the service was unavailable. Throwing on shoes and a jacket, he ran out the door to see what was happening for himself—and to find Zoey.

Leon didn't have to drive for long before he witnessed the carnage occurring throughout the city. As he drove slowly down Pine Street, Leon saw a woman about 200 yards ahead jogging quickly in his direction. He stopped the car in the middle of the road. Something moving. A figure scurried after the woman.

Along the second story outer wall, Leon watched the figure skitter with spider-like grace along the side of the building, like an enormous arachnid, holding on to the crevices within the brickwork. It stalked the woman, kept pace with its prey. When the creature was ready, it pounced. Pinned to the ground, the woman was powerless to flee.

She screamed, "No! No! Let me go."

The creature restrained her, clawed fingers ripped at her flesh. Shock registered across her face as she bellowed louder, "No! Daniel, no!"

Obviously she knew her attacker, but it was too late. Leon watched as the creature tore off a piece of her shoulder with his teeth. Blood splattered across the building wall as the undead Daniel fed on his companion. Sudden movement caught Leon's eye.

A glimmer of steel sparked in the lamplight as an enormous man emerged from the gloom wielding a machete. There was no hesitation, no second thought in his actions. With a single blow, his blade decapitated Daniel's head. The man knelt and examined the battered woman. Her body was broken and beyond saving.

Dread weighed on Leon's shoulders as he observed the deep lines etched on the man's brow. Even from a few car lengths away, he viewed the color drain from the man's face. The man rose and tightened the grip on his machete. His other hand ran through his hair and wiped at his eyes. Leon stood motionless as he viewed the man hoist the machete high above his head and hesitate a moment. Leon swore the man's mouth mumbled a prayer. Steel sliced the air before it severed the woman's head from her body.

Leon's stomach lurched. He pitched his head out the window while he released the contents of his stomach. His face burned with heat and his eyes watered as Leon continued to fight for breath and his stomach convulsed. Once finished, he hung his head, sucking in a few ragged breaths.

Leon wiped his mouth with his jacket sleeve. He peered down the street. The man lingered near the dead woman's body, his mouth curved downward in a frown. As Leon looked past the man, he saw a mass of bodies coming down the hill toward them. On further observation, he suspected the crowd was no longer among the living. The horde converged faster than suspected and there was no way Leon could reach the man before the group was close enough to rip them apart. He jerked the gear shift into reverse and slammed on the gas, leaving the man to fend for himself.

Tires squealed and rubber burned across the road as Leon spun the car in the opposite direction. He stomped on the gas pedal and glanced in the rear-view mirror as the car accelerated. Someone rushed out from a nearby building a short distance from the undead horde. The mass descended on the young man before he had a chance to react.

Leon heard screams as he maneuvered up the road away from the scene. Eyes glued to the rear-view mirror, the sun sat low in the sky. Gray-blue clouds drifted in the sky and melded into deep yellows and oranges. Twilight was a bloom as carnage filled the streets.

Leon drove away, his heart heavy with the horror he had witnessed within such proximity. Tears streamed down his face as anger brewed inside himself. This isn't what he'd imagined, but could it be the answer he was looking for all along? Could he sway the outcome? The uncertainty enraged him. Leon wasn't concerned about the people who were lost, but about his legacy, which seemed out of his control. He was certain some of the fallen were his colleagues. In his line of research, he didn't have many friends, but his thoughts drifted to Zoey. Was she okay?

Nothing would ever be the same again.

Once Leon was out of danger, he pressed hard on the brakes and rammed the gear into park. His chin dropped to his chest. *Shit.* He trembled and fought the rising panic consuming him. The cell phone lay at his feet. He grabbed it and tried Zoey's number. A high-pitched buzz and then nothing. Service was out.

He raised his head and looked around. Leon noticed movement in a nearby alleyway—three people huddled together, their faces grim and eyes wide with fear. They were obviously survivors like him. He opened the glove compartment and retrieved his Staccato CS, the handgun he'd never fired, but now seemed like a suitable time to keep the pistol nearby. His hands shook as he checked the magazine and safety before awkwardly placing it in his waistband.

One of the trio yelled in his direction and walked toward him holding a piece of wood by his side. "What do you want?"

Leon cracked the window a few inches and answered, "Drove away from the city center. Getting my bearings is all." Leon gave a quick smile and put his hands up so they could see he wasn't injured or a threat. His hands quivered like he was a cheerleader doing spirit-fingers before he noticed, clenching his fingers together quickly to make fists.

The survivors nodded in understanding before introducing themselves.

"I'm Ray, this is my wife, Carla, and my brother, Jerry. We were part of a larger group of people escaping the mall at the other end of Grand Avenue. Our family unit had been hurrying from building to building, away from the large mass of creatures. We separated from the others while escaping a couple of those undead people. That's what the reporters are calling them anyway, undead people."

The young woman extended her hand. "Hi, I'm Carla, happy to see a normal face. You're welcome to join us. We'd appreciate a lift if your car can get us out of town faster."

Leon hesitated for a moment, feeling a mix of emotions. He was anxious and weary after the events of the night, but the thought of having company and being able to help his fellow survivors gave him courage. He took Carla's hand. With a nod of agreement, he invited them into the car. "I'll drive wherever you need me to go," he said.

The group devised a plan as they drove. They would make their way to a nearby grocery store and scavenge what supplies were left behind before heading out of town to find a safe place. They'd rest for the night before attempting to locate the lost members of their group.

Leon smiled. Despite all that had happened, he felt refreshed by their enthusiasm, inspired by their resilience and determination in the face of such devastating circumstances. Together they could find food and supplies - together they could survive.

"Why do you need to meet up with the rest of the group from the mall?" Leon asked as he pulled into a food mart near the edge of the city and parked the car. It was quiet, nothing out of place. It appeared as though the horrors of Lindaire Hills had not reached the food mart. At least not yet.

Ray helped Carla out of the backseat and turned to Leon. "We're not actually married. Our family was together to help us pick out our wedding attire. We were supposed to get married tomorrow at the courthouse. Both of our parents, grandparents, and Carla's sister are somewhere still in the mall or in the city."

Jerry slammed a fist on the hood of the car, causing everyone to jump. "Dammit, we can't leave! We gotta go back and find everyone. They're not going to make it on their own."

Leon watched the exchange among his new companions. Carla slipped away from Jerry and cowered behind Ray. Her chin was down, but her eyes were laser-focused on Jerry. Leon sensed the family may not be as close as first impressions implied. He shuffled farther back to take in the interactions. Carla wrapped her hands over her abdomen. It could be a defensive gesture, but Leon wondered if it meant more.

"I know, brother, I know. We need a plan, and we can't wait until tomorrow," Ray said. He took a step toward his brother and Carla grabbed his bicep in response. Ray froze. "Blowing up and banging on shit isn't going to make it easier. Jerry, you know you get spun-up and spiral when you're pissed. Let's gather supplies and go back. It'll be easier with the car. Just chill."

Leon's mind traveled back to the mention of a wedding and his thoughts shifted to Zoey. *Where are you?* He couldn't leave her alone to face this madness either. "You're right. We can't wait until tomorrow. My fiancée is somewhere in the city, too. I say we grab whatever we can inside and go back. I'll get you all as close to your family as I can, then I'm going to search for Zoey. My apartment isn't too far from where I met you. Find your people and you can hole up with us until you figure out what to do next. Anyone's phone still work?"

Carla cringed. Her fingers tightened around Ray's arm. "No, calls aren't getting through. If we manage to connect, it cuts off seconds later."

Leon nodded and popped the trunk. He fished out a flashlight from a rusty toolbox. "Let's grab what we can and get back to the city. Time is of the essence."

CHAPTER FIVE

The group entered the food mart to grab supplies and confirm Carla's suggestion that no calls were getting through. Inside was a stark contrast to the unscathed exterior. Inside the convenience store was utter disorder. The narrow shelves were almost cleared out of useful items. A few glass jars were shattered from an end cap, the contents melding together in a congealed blob on the tile. Canned goods lay scattered across an isle floor. A television mounted on the wall behind the counter was reporting the weather.

Leon watched Jerry strut toward a door that said Employees Only and disappear behind the door. A faint noise followed before the door slammed closed. Leon stood in front of the checkout counter and shook his head. He noticed the television screen change from reporting the weather to an emergency alert. He was reading the information at the bottom of the screen when Jerry came out of the room with keys jingling from a finger raised in the air. Leon was curious why this new acquaintance was buttoning his shirt sleeve with his other hand until Leon spotted blood seeping through the fabric near the man's elbow.

Leon turned away and tossed his chin up toward the television. "Lindaire Falls is falling apart and they're broadcasting a weather report."

Jerry stopped alongside Leon. "This is some fucked up shit. Am I right?" He jabbed a shoulder into Leon's side as he spoke.

A knot formed in Leon's stomach. "It sure is."

"Whoever started this mess …"

Leon held his tongue and walked away, leaving Jerry to stare at the screen by himself.

The rest of the group quickly made their way to different aisles, collecting whatever they could find — canned foods, juice boxes, and other snacks for energy during their search, bandages and medical supplies in case any of them got hurt.

The day had taken its toll on all of them. Guilt and fear clung to Leon as he grabbed items off the shelves—what if they couldn't find Zoey? He didn't realize he'd whispered her name until he felt a hand touch his shoulder. Carla smiled reassuringly before squeezing his arm. "We'll all help."

Jerry yelled, "You piece of shit!" He emerged around the corner of the aisle, his shoulders hunched, and his face scrunched into a crimson grimace as he stomped toward Leon. One finger was inches from Leon's face while the other hand's fingers squeezed a small box. "Why are the police looking for you? Wanting to question you? Your picture is all over the news. Did you start this fucked up mess?"

Leon retreated as Jerry pressed forward.

Carla recoiled. Her hand fell from Leon's shoulder as her eyes darted between the two men.

Ray heard his brother from an aisle away. "Damn it, Jerry." He turned the corner and put a protective arm around Carla as he eyed the two men.

"No!" Leon exclaimed as he receded a step. "I—I didn't start this." He crept farther back until he felt the cold glass of the refrigerated case hit his shoulder blades. His chest heaved with each gulp of air. The whites of his eyes bulged with tiny red veins zigzagging at the corners.

Jerry whispered to Ray as his gaze bore into Leon.

Leon shifted his eyes to Carla, searching for sympathy. He noted confusion and worry, but sympathy was nowhere to be found.

Ray put a hand over Jerry's and said, "No."

Leon pulled in a deep breath. "I was at the women's prison before the outbreak. That may be why the police are searching for me."

"Why were you at the women's prison?" Jerry asked.

"I'm a doctor. I was on call to help whenever they needed me to fill in." Leon glanced at Jerry, then Carla and Ray as they stood side-by-side absorbing every word he spoke. "You don't believe me?"

"Not really." Jerry said.

"The truth is," he continued, "I'm the head of research at Aionios Pharmaceuticals. If the police want to talk to me, it could be a number of reasons. I was at the prison where this outbreak was thought to have started. I also have access to contagions and viruses, as many research facilities do."

Carla tilted her head as she raised an eyebrow. "So you are behind this."

"No," Leon lied, but his gut churned in alarm.

"Bullshit." Jerry slid close, pinning Leon against the cold glass. "You're a lying sack of shit."

"Jer, knock it off!" Carla pulled Jerry's arm, catching him off balance. He staggered a few paces as she stepped between the two men. "Stop being an ass. This man helped us. He could have left us out there, but he didn't."

Jerry's cheeks flushed and his face contorted as he righted himself and leaned into Carla's face. "He's lying. I know it." Jerry spat as he spoke, spittle landing on Carla's cheek.

Carla's eyes flared as she wiped the muck off with her shirt sleeve. "Maybe, but you are a narcissistic prick."

Ray wrenched Carla from between the two men. "Enough, Carla."

Jerry pulled back his hand holding a block of soap and slammed it into Leon's face.

A loud crack and blood gushed from Leon's nose, pouring down his chin.

Leon staggered. The back of his head whipped against the glass door then forward. He fell against Jerry, grabbing at anything as the man pushed Leon off him. Leon caught a shirt sleeve and ripped it away as he fell to the floor with a thud.

Ray grabbed his brother. "He ain't worth it. We gotta get out of here and find our family."

"I wasn't aiming for him," Jerry said. His eyes were smoldering sockets, staring at Carla. "But he deserved it."

Ray shoved Jerry into the shelves. "You are a prick, but you're my brother. Knock it off so we can get out of here and find Mom and the others."

CHAPTER SIX

FAMILY TIES

Leon sat on the dirty tiled floor as the others filled bags with items and trudged back and forth between the car and the store. He stayed where he had landed, tending to his nose after an excruciating attempt to reset it. He'd found a package of hand wipes on a shelf and cleaned the blood from his face after his nostrils stopped oozing a trail down the crease left by a scar over his lip. Blood covered his shirt, the metallic aroma fresh and intense.

As he tended to his wounds, he had decided to separate from the others. Although Ray and Carla appeared to be normal friendly folks, Leon knew Jerry would be a constant threat. He had the pistol, but what good was it if they ganged up on him and forced his hand? Better to leave them here where they had some chance to find their family.

After twenty minutes he stood and grabbed a travel-size package of aspirin. Leon popped the pills in his mouth. He heard a thump as if someone fell to the floor, then a shriek, and rush of movement.

Leon stumbled around the corner, aspirin bottle still in hand. In his blurry vision he saw his companions struggling atop another figure splayed across the parking lot just outside the open entrance. Its grotesquely pale hands clawed toward Carla's face. She screamed. Her arms flailed as she tried to break free. Ray had one arm wrapped tightly around Jerry's shoulders pulling him off the creature. Ray had a broomstick pointed toward the attacker's temple.

Carla turned as another creature lurched toward her. She ran into the store and grasped a child-size baseball bat from a display by the pinball machine. Turning quickly, she shoved it back into the lot with the tip of the bat, and pummeled the ghoul until she knocked it off its feet.

The sight snapped Leon out of his daze. Shock, quickly followed by rage, flushed through him like an electric current. Every nerve ending ignited as he charged forward, roaring wildly at what lay before him. Bright yellow containers on a nearby shelf caught his eye. He grabbed two of them, hitting the caps on the aisle corner until they popped off. Leon chucked the open bottles at the creature Carla had knocked to the ground. He watched as the lighter fluid raced out, the containers twisted in the wind until he hit his mark. The liquid gurgled out of the bottles. Not his best throw but it would do the job.

As the undead struggled to rise, Leon waved his hands at Carla, thrashing and screaming for her and the others to clear the doorway. Leaving no time for explanations, he bellowed, "Run!" His voice was charged with adrenaline. Leon pulled the gun from his waistband as he passed by them and squeezed off a round, aiming for the metal trash bin near his mark.

The shot echoed through the store as Leon watched the spark catch. Flames erupted, engulfing the creature. It roared a guttural screech as its arms reached out. Leon aimed again and fired a round into the monster's skull. It fell with a thud onto the parking lot asphalt. As he caught his breath, a shuffle from behind made him whirl around. The creature Jerry and Ray had been fighting crawled toward Leon. Its leg broken, a protruding tibia scraped the ground as it pulled itself closer to him. Leon slowly released a deep breath and squeezed the trigger, landing a shot into the eye socket. The creature's head was a mess of grisly remains, dripping with fleshy bits, its eye a beehive of bone shards and blood splatter. It groaned, dragging itself closer to Leon.

Leon's nostrils curled as a sweet, coppery scent of rotting blood filled the air.

The smell of iron and gunpowder sent Leon's head spinning. The stench recalled distant memories Leon sought to banish. When he was ten and his father had taken him hunting, forcing him to shoot a white-tail deer. His father's prideful clasp on his shoulder put Leon to his knees. Then, lifted as if he were a feather, father and son followed the blood trail until they found the gorgeous creature struggling to breathe, blood pink and bubbly trickling down its fur. Leon gagged at the wretched memory, bile burning his throat.

"Leon!"

Carla's scream interrupted his thoughts. The creature had reached his feet and was yanking at Leon's pant leg. Leon recoiled. His body went stiff with dread. A shiver ran through him as he stepped back and aimed at what once was a young woman's face. A vaguely familiar eye remained. Uneasy, he quickly targeted the forehead and squeezed the trigger. Despite the bullet's velocity, the seconds before impact ticked by slowly. Leon's finger pressure on the trigger now a steady, thumping beat, he removed his finger and eased the pistol to his side. Absentminded, his gaze registered the bits of skull, brain matter, and blood staining his pant leg.

"You had a fucking gun all this time?" Jerry stormed toward Leon.

"Jerry! Enough! He just saved our asses." Ray intercepted his brother, shoving him away from Leon.

Jerry raised his hands then shuffled back into the store shaking his head.

Carla held her stomach as Ray turned to her and wrapped an arm around her. "How are you and the bean holding up? Everything okay?"

"You're pregnant?" Leon asked.

"Yes, about six months now," Ray answered with pride in his voice. "Our first."

Leon frowned and gazed at the carnage by his feet. He closed his eyes and drew in a long slow breath and let it out, then took another.

"What's the problem? Why does my pregnancy upset you?" Carla curled herself tight against Ray, her arms squeezing around his waist.

Leon released a huff. "Have you been bitten? Either of you? Any type of wound—check now."

"No. Why?" Ray asked. His eyes wide as he stood straight and looked over Carla's body.

"What is going to happen to my baby?" Carla asked, her voice shaky as a single tear trailed down her cheek.

"Quickly. Go inside—in the restroom and scrutinize each other for any wounds, especially bite marks. Don't go into the office. I think an infected may be in that room. If clean, you must leave Jerry behind. He's been bitten."

"Are you out of your fucking mind?" Ray screamed.

Leon put a finger to his lips. "Shh. You must listen. Go check and I'll explain after. Jerry is coming."

Jerry strolled toward them with a tallboy can of beer to his lips. Four more dangled from the plastic strap of a six-pack. Where Leon had torn Jerry's shirt sleeve earlier, dark blood oozed from a single bite mark on his arm. It wasn't deep but Leon could tell the infection was slowly spreading through Jerry's system. Black tendrils branching out from the wound under discolored flesh fascinated Leon.

Carla placed her hands on her hips and rolled her eyes. "Really, Jer? Now is not the time for one of your drunken stupors."

"Now is the perfect time, and I'll fucking drink whenever I want."

Leon cleared his throat. "The bathroom is on the right past the office door."

Ray nodded. He steered Carla past his brother, giving a wide berth. Ray cringed at the sight of Jerry's blackened and bloody forearm. He mouthed a silent prayer and motioned the sign of the cross.

A few minutes later, with an arm wrapped around his fiancée's shoulder, Ray and Carla trudged out from the store's narrow hallway in the back. As Ray passed his brother, a storm crossed his face, deep lines filled with disdain as Jerry sat on the floor drinking number four from the six-pack. Ray shifted his eyes to find Leon and steered Carla in Leon's direction.

Leon saw the couple emerge and waited until they were close enough that he could speak in a whisper. "So, what's the verdict?"

"We're okay."

"Good." Leon hung his head.

"What's the problem?" Carla asked. She put a hand on his arm.

"You two must leave, now. Jerry's not safe." Leon shook his head. "I hate to ask this, since he's your brother, but we need to secure—"

"What do you mean by secure?" Ray interrupted with a hard edge.

"I have a rope in the trunk of the car. Help me tie him up to a chair or something and then you both should go. Nothing good can come from you staying until his end. I'll wait and make sure he doesn't hurt anyone else." Leon observed Ray's face transform from anger to reluctant resolution.

"What makes you so sure he's beyond saving?" Ray asked.

Leon shrugged. "I don't know how long it will take, but I am certain it's throughout his bloodstream. I suspect the store clerk is in that office and attacked Jerry when he opened the door. Either way, the creature's DNA has been running in his system for at least an hour. It's hit every vital organ." He noticed their heads bob as each piece of information made sense.

"Ray, he's right. We can't risk it." Carla slid her hand into his and gave it a squeeze.

"I know he's an asshole, but I didn't see this coming." Ray's head hung low as he scuffed a shoe over the blacktop. Leon's words took root, weaving through every scenario in his mind. Ray's chest heaved as he stifled a choked sob. His eyes met Carla's as a tear slid down his cheek.

"I know, baby." Carla put her hand on his shoulder. "This sucks."

Ray took in a long breath and held it. The air hissed as it escaped through clenched teeth. He straightened his shoulders and said, "All right, let's get this over with."

Leon and Ray noticed Jerry sat with his head resting against the wall as they came around the corner of the sales counter. A beer tilted in his hand, dripping its contents onto Jerry's thigh and the floor. He was mumbling, eyes droopy, and drool hanging from the left corner of his mouth. Leon noted the dark lines under Jerry's skin spreading above his shirt collar. Several more beer cans scattered the dirty tile.

"It's spreading quickly," Leon said as he leaned toward Ray. "We need to secure him now."

"Jerry, come on, man. The world's going to shit and you can't pass up a drink." Ray shook his head as he moved toward his brother. He reached for Jerry's arm, the one not bitten but covered now with dark webbing under the skin. "Doc, you got that side? Let's get him in the chair."

They lifted Jerry and secured him to a swivel chair with rope Leon had pulled from his car. Leon tied Jerry's arms as Ray got his legs.

Carla watched from the entrance, hugging the slight bump of her belly. She whipped her head toward the parking lot. "Someone's coming."

"Go to Carla. I'll move Jerry."

Leon rolled Jerry into the office and closed the door behind him. His gaze fell on the body behind the desk, its head and mouth wrapped in duct tape, arms tied to chair arms, similar to Jerry's. It squirmed, moaning A beer and tape were on the desk. Leon touched the beer, still cool. "Guess we know how you got bitten now, don't we?" Leon said under his breath. He looked at Jerry passed out. Leon stepped out and closed the door.

As Ray pulled Carla close, a young man drove by at a crawl, peering into the store. When the man's line of sight caught Ray's eye, the driver sped up and swung out onto the road, speeding away.

"Just a kid looking for trouble. He's gone." Ray shouted to Leon as his arm tightened around Carla, giving her a reassuring smile.

"You both should go now. I'll monitor Jerry until he isn't Jerry anymore," Leon said as he stepped up alongside the couple.

"I want to say goodbye to my brother," Ray said with a hitch to his voice.

"It's best you not. We don't need him to get agitated and bite you or have you come in contact with his wound. We don't know if a simple touch can spread this contagion."

Carla gasped and rubbed her stomach. "Don't go, babe. I need you. We need you safe."

"There's another body in there. A body that's clearly dead, but still moves. A beer is on the desk. I think Jerry had a run-in with that thing when he went into the office. He got himself bitten and then tied it up. It's the only scenario that makes sense."

"I need to see him."

Leon nodded, "Stay at the doorway, for your own protection."

Leon waved as Ray and Carla drove off, leaving him with his medical bag and a few supplies from the car. The couple kept his pistol.

He gave them his address in case they needed shelter in the city. He'd find Zoey and meet them there. Leon watched as they drove back toward the city's center to locate their family. He closed the store doors and tied them shut, then pushed a game machine and shelving to cover the double glass doors of the front entrance. No one was going to get through without considerable effort.

Satisfied with the latch guard on the remaining door at the rear of the building, Leon took his time going to the office. He hadn't had a moment to himself since meeting the trio and realized he was famished.

He took inventory of his options and, with a gleeful smile, pulled items from the shelves and coolers to make a picnic.

CHAPTER SEVEN

CURIOSITY

Leon rubbed an achy shoulder as he righted himself. Clearing the sleep from his eyes, he jumped up, realizing the rest of the evening had gone by and thick darkness settled in around the store. He hurried to the counter and checked his phone. Two in the morning. He'd slept for hours. He had wanted to conduct his analysis and be far away from this place before dawn. Now, pressed for time, he had to choose between continuing with his studies or venturing to his apartment in the inky unknown of night.

Fascinated by research, his choice was obvious.

With his tools splayed out across the desk, Leon ignored Jerry's grumbling murmurs. He couldn't wait a moment longer. The virus had spread from the bite on his arm through Jerry's body as Leon slept. It weaved a hideous pattern across Jerry's face and down the opposite side of his body from the bite wound.

The infection was far more advanced than Leon had wanted to conduct his analysis, but the situation would have to do.

Leon plucked the tape from Jerry's mouth and asked, "Anything you'd like to say or have me write down for a message to your loved ones? Ray perhaps? You don't have much time left."

"What the fuck is wrong with you, man?" Jerry asked. Tape residue stretched like tiny ribbons of spider web as he spoke. He licked his swollen, cracked lips and opened his mouth wide several times.

Leon remained calm. "Wrong with me? Nothing. You have the virus rushing through your body from the bite on your arm. Ray and Carla left hours ago. You're in my care until your end."

"Care, my ass." Jerry squirmed against the restraints holding his arms to the chair back. "Untie me."

"I cannot do that."

"Why the fuck not?"

"I'll be blunt. Your heart rate is extremely high but weak, which tells me your muscles are becoming rigid. You do know your heart is a giant muscle?"

"Thuck you," Jerry mumbled. His deep brown eyes rolled with annoyance. "I'm not an idiothh. Whath the thuck?"

"That's your speech going. Soon you'll either have a heart attack or slowly suffocate before you die, then sometime after that, you'll turn into him." Leon waved a finger toward the remnants of the store clerk writhing in the other chair. "I told Ray I'd stay with you until you died, and make sure you didn't turn into one of these undead necrotic creatures."

Leon couldn't help but reflect on his time in medical school as he and his classmates looked upon a research cadaver. He'd been unimpressed by the gray lifeless tunnels of the human brain. The lack of fresh tissue to observe and delve into for study unnerved him in an inexplicable way.

How he'd longed for the opportunity to observe brain surgery. To witness the vibrant and intricate neural network as it was poked and prodded, forcing the synapses to fire on command.

An ugly sneer crossed his lips as his eyes darted back and forth between the two specimens in the store office. The opportunity to observe both worlds lay at his fingertips.

Leon absently watched Jerry's eyes bulge as his turned neck strained to keep his head up and eyes focused on the animated corpse. As Jerry's head fell, Leon knew realization had set in.

Leon moved toward the tools spread across the office desk. "I'm going to study the change as best I can, comparing his brain," Leon tapped the store clerk's skull with the end of a small rotary saw, "to yours."

The silver glint of the saw shone in the light. A part of his medical kit for decades, Leon had never had a reason to use the bone saw. His heart raced at the thought of using the instrument. His mind's eye envisioned the procedure, chiseling into the flesh and bone to reveal the body's workhorse, the human brain. A smile played at his lips.

Jerry jerked, unable to lift his head but a few inches. He turned a canted chin toward Leon. Jerry's lids twitched as he tried to keep his eyes open. "Fu-fu'er."

Leon released a bitter laugh. "Perhaps I am that and more." He ignored Jerry's incoherent mumblings as he set to work. The grinding of the rotary saw against the dead's flesh released a buildup of foul gases from rot. Putrefaction had set in, rendering the tissue a sickly shade of gray-green, with patches of necrotic lesions scattered across the surface. Once the large fragment of scalp was removed, Leon marveled at the specimen's brain, once a complex organ orchestrating thoughts and emotions, now presented a ghastly spectacle of decay and deterioration.

Although Leon believed the store clerk to be nothing more than an average or below average man, the stillness of the brain unnerved him. Leon pressed on the cerebellum, the only region to show a faint pulse, a jerking motion that coincided with the body's awkward gestures and truncated thrashing. The hippocampus, responsible for recollection and navigation, appeared as a diminished relic, unable to retain a fraction of the individual's human essence. According to the news reporter, the creatures recognized family or loved ones. Leon pondered if this portion of the brain strained to maintain autonomy once infection set it, but diminished as time wore on to the dull husk Leon saw before him.

Suddenly the decay and stench overwhelmed Leon as his stomach violently rolled and pitched. He swallowed the bile that rose to the back of his throat. A heavy breath and then another, held the contents of his stomach in check. He grabbed the small canister of menthol ointment from his bag and rubbed a generous amount under his nostrils.

Working quickly, he tapped Jerry on the shoulder, back, and then on his head with significant force. Concerned at the lack of response, Leon came around from behind Jerry and squatted in front of the man.

Jerry's eyes flickered as Leon lifted his chin. "Are you still with me?" Leon asked. "Don't leave me yet. I'm going to start now. Not that I think you can feel anything."

A flash of rage danced across Jerry's eyes and then vanished as a low growling drone came from his chest.

"I see you're more than alert. That's good!" Leon stood and rushed to where he'd been, ready for the second part of his analysis. He grabbed the rotary saw with bits of bone and hair from the store clerk still in the saw's jagged teeth and clicked the switch. Keeping his tools sterile and in pristine condition was of little consequence at the moment.

The buzz of the blade generated a hollow whirling in the tiny room. The fangs of the diamond-cut steel edge gnawed through Jerry's skull with ruthless purpose. As he cracked through the inner crust of cranial bone, blood spurted out, coating Leon's chest in a warm, crimson wave.

Leon hummed as the saw snapped through the final edge, creating a circular, hair-covered disc to remove. "How are you doing, Jerry?"

He was answered with a quick murmur.

"Excellent. Let's see what we have here." Leon removed the bone disc and placed it on the desk behind him. He heard his grandfather's voice.

You know what that looks like, doncha, boy? A chip off the old block after all.

"Shut up, Grandpa. I'm nothing like you."

All evidence to the contrary.

"Shut up!" Leon said in a huff.

He turned and focused on the pink-hued tissue emanating from Jerry's head. Leon dabbed away blood that pooled along the rim.

Leon marveled at the wondrous comparison. The pulsating vitality of a living brain alongside its necrotic counterpart exuding an eerie stillness, a silent testament to the absence of cognitive processes. The synapses, once conduits of intricate communication, now lay dormant or misfiring, creating chaotic and unpredictable patterns.

What was once the seat of consciousness and self-awareness had transformed into a grotesque mockery of its former self. The cerebellum, crucial for motor control, showed signs of degeneration, resulting in awkward and uncoordinated movements. Neural pathways, now disrupted and fractured, contributed to the unhuman-human's relentless pursuit of a singular instinct: the consumption of the living. Leon pondered. *Is there more to this instinct? Is it a primal desire for blood to rush through their body—the warmth now absent so they feed to gather a glimmer, no matter how fleeting, of their former selves? It's an unreachable answer I fear science too cannot explain.*

"You need to do more research, boy."

Leon startled at his father's voice, so prominent in his mind. He could almost feel his father's breath at the back of his ear.

"Father, this was a rare opportunity. It cannot be repeated, nor would I dare contemplate such a notion," Leon said.

"Just as your grandpa taught me. You cannot stop something you started. You must finish this to the end."

"But this is not what I started. This is something else. Intriguing, perplexing, and, of course, worthy of investigation, but not to continue like this. We need answers to find a cure. To unhinge this madness—put the genie back in the bottle!"

Science demands sacrifice!

Leon shivered as his grandfather's voice bellowed from the depths of his mind. He struggled with the right response. His conscience was raging a war against itself. Yet Leon felt his insides tighten each time he contemplated continuing to follow his grandfather's ways. All his life he'd pursued science to win the approval of his father. As he gazed over the bedlam he'd unleashed in this very room, Leon realized he'd been seeking approval from his grandfather's ghost. A vile phantom of World War II, lost to the foolishness of an imprudent leader.

"It's not sacrifice if we are inflicting harm on others for our own gain. That's simply madness," Leon said.

MADNESS?

Leon jolted and cupped his cheek, the deep baritone voice of his grandfather erupting in his mind. Coupled with the memory of the old man's jarring slap, Leon winced as if he'd received one that instant. If he didn't know better, he'd swear he felt the heat of his cheek radiating through his fingers.

The air was suddenly thick with a sickening aroma of decay, a repulsive symphony assaulting his senses. A noxious blend of rotting flesh and the soppy-sweet undertones of decomposing tissues permeated the small room.

Leon rushed out the door, hoping to find fresher air in the main storeroom. The scent lingered like a crushing fog, assaulting his nostrils with an unsettling intensity he feared was also certainly unforgettable.

The second wave forcing Leon over a trash can was a sharp, acrid stench reminiscent of ammonia. He knew it was the result of proteins breaking down into rancescent compounds, yet his intelligence couldn't dispel the overwhelming need to vomit. The odor cut through the air, inducing a spontaneous convulsion as the offensive smell clung to his every breath.

He shook his head from side to side, seeking to clear his senses of not only the rotting stench, but the visions and voices of his father and grandfather lingering still at the periphery.

To avoid smelling his own breath as he regained his composure, Leon clenched his jaw tight. His lips remained pursed in a horrid expression as he breathed in and out, cautious to gain his composure and control of his spasmodic abdominal muscles.

After a minute or two, Leon stood on wobbly legs. The disturbing voices ripped away any further interest in investigating the brain compositions of his specimens. Leon felt defeat with each cautious step, and then another toward the office, now ripe with decomposition and rot wafting out the doorway.

He had to put an end to their misery. He did promise Ray he would ensure Jerry did not remain one of the undead. Yet years as a researcher were ingrained in Leon's psyche, to have the unanswerable answered—to grasp the opportunity for discovery.

Leon hesitated as he again stood behind Jerry and what remained of the office clerk. He pondered if the stench had escaped out the opening or if he'd now become used to the stench. He drew a wary breath, slow and deliberate. Leon noticed a change in the air, a sick sweetness lingered. It was heavy, like the weight of the horror surrounding him.

A thought hit Leon. He would not soon forget this particular moment. The visions and voices of his father and grandfather weighed immensely as Leon took a long moment before stabbing the last moving remnants of the office clerk's brain. What remained of the creature let out a raspy gasp, before its head slumped forward.

Jerry remained still. Leon pulled Jerry's head back slightly and was met with bulging eyes. They twitched from side to side as Leon felt for a pulse along the man's neck, finding none.

Time moves on.

Leon pictured his mother as she was when he last heard her voice, a sense of relief playing at the end of her words. They'd stood hand-in-hand in front of his grandfather's casket. She'd looked down at his boyish frame and asked why he was holding his cheek.

"It's where PopPop would slap me when I wasn't listening to him," Leon recalled, his face flush with embarrassment.

His mother bent down, pulled his hand away and kissed the heat rising where his palm had been. "You need not worry about that any longer. He can't hurt you ever again."

Looks like PopPop found a way, Momma.

Jerry's body jerked.

Leon bounced back against the desk in surprise. The clatter of his instruments hitting the floor ricocheted off the walls.

A low groan, like a hideous humming, purred from Jerry's chest as he fought against the restraints.

Leon stood tall and peered into what remained of Jerry's brain. What was a haphazard patchwork of thick gray-pink tissue was dark and shriveled. All but the cerebellum, which still writhed and pulsed with synaptic movement. He'd made a promise. Leon selected a slender tool from the mangle of instruments on the floor and jabbed the tip into what remained of Jerry's mind.

"It is done."

CHAPTER EIGHT

WALKING

Leon had loaded a child-size backpack with water and supplies. He'd locked the office and left a sign that read 'Don't Enter! Creatures inside.' Once he wrote it, he debated about tossing it in the trash, but pinned it to the door anyway. He snatched a baseball cap from the countertop stand and adjusted it to fit his head. Two days of stubble did little to cover his features, and he needed to shield his face since his picture had been plastered all over the news. He grabbed the tools and medical bag before leaving the convenience store. After trying to call Zoey with no success, he walked in the direction of his apartment. He'd try her again when he was safe in his own space. Maybe the landline was working.

The sun was shining with a cool breeze in the air. He calculated it was about five miles to travel on foot to his apartment, but with no idea who or what he would run into, the trip could take much longer than normal. Leon made a quick mental note—the lab was on the way from this direction.

He'd waited outside the store for ten or fifteen minutes, studying the surroundings for movement, taking precautions to avoid immediate encounters with people or creatures. Not a creature stirred. And it was quiet, like life was void in every direction. Even the birds seemed to have forgotten how to sing.

Deep in thought, Leon walked for a mile without seeing or hearing anything other than the intimidating groan of trees bending in the soft breeze. The quietness unnerved him. He felt the tension rising in his body and his shoulders were tight. The pack hung low on his back. He lifted the straps as he twisted and stretched, working the muscles loose. He lowered the backpack to the ground and dropped his medical bag.

Leon stepped into the tree line, in between two prickly ash shrubs at the entrance of the city park to relieve himself. As he turned back toward the street and took a few steps, someone grabbed him from behind.

A smell fixed in his nostrils as he twisted and caught an arm, tearing at an orange sleeve as he tumbled over his dropped bags. The thick leather strap of his medical bag caught the perpetrator's hand, and they jerked to free themselves in the scuffle. His bag landed with a thud on the street.

A guttural shriek near his ear jolted him as a head of long dirty-blond hair streaked with pink flung up toward his neck. He ducked and rolled under an arm to come up behind the person and pushed hard on their back. They fell to the ground with a groan and turned over.

A woman. At least that's what she used to be, dressed in an orange jumpsuit. Leon's insides tightened as he peered at how she'd turned into one of *them*. She wasn't human anymore. Her skin was a pale olive hue, with scrapes and nail marks. Leon mused he wasn't the first to fight off her attacks. She had a few teeth missing. Bloody sockets indicated the teeth had come out recently and would not heal.

She twisted like a pretzel, her fingers splayed out, clawing toward Leon's leg.

He kicked her in the shoulder, forcing her head to bounce from the pavement.

Unphased, she bolted up and lurched toward him, her arms and legs contorting like a horrid dance of morbidity.

Fear and anger flooded Leon. His eyes wide, he flung himself at her, knocking her to the ground as he scrambled to remain standing. His foot came down on her shoulder. He heard a sharp crack.

She reached across with the other arm as Leon's leg raised over her head. Fueled from an inner rage he didn't understand, Leon slammed the heel of his shoe into her nose. Blood, burgundy and rancid, spurt from her face as she howled like an animal caught in a trap. He lifted his foot again, and again, until there was nothing left of her face.

Stunned by his actions, Leon recoiled from the wreckage and sucked in a deep, shaky breath. He trembled as sweat dripped down his back.

Leon sat on the curb, staring at the carnage he had inflicted on the woman. A necrotic vessel, nothing more than a rabid animal. A woman he'd twisted into a primal monster that had attacked him. Rabid—could it be that he'd created a radical form of rabies? Chemical formulas and equations flitted through his mind. It was no use—the answer was out of reach.

Guilt tugged at his heart.

Maybe I am like my father and grandfather after all?

Thoughts drifted to his mother, Lina, as she sat with him one fall morning many years ago. It was a day or two before she had died, and she had prodded his twelve-year-old self to talk about what he wanted to be when he grew up.

"I guess I'll be a scientific engineer like Dad. That's all he talks about, following in his footsteps."

She didn't respond right away, letting the cool wind and rustling of fall leaves fill the silence. Her thin arm wrapped around Leon's shoulders, and she gave him a gentle squeeze.

"You don't have to do that if you don't want to, you know. If you could choose a career in anything at all, what would you like to be?" she asked.

"Anything?" He remembered the excitement in his voice. "I'd be a doctor and cure terrible diseases, like what has made you sick." His chest puffed out as he looked into his mother's gray eyes for approval.

He remembered seeing a tear slide from the corner of her eye.

"Momma?"

"I'm okay, sweetie." she said. "That's a fine profession, Leon. If that's what you want, don't let anyone stand in your way. Not even your father."

The scrape and thump of something coming from behind him made Leon jump.

A gunshot blasted past Leon's head as he turned. He ducked, screaming as he squatted down.

A man, or what was left of him, lay across the road's shoulder. Half the face was gone, yet the body jerked and twisted on the ground.

A man in camouflage rushed past Leon and slammed an axe into what was left of a man's face. Once, twice, and then the beating stopped. Blood covered the attacker's face and arms.

Leon thanked the man and received a gruff grunt in reply. "You should walk away from the city, not toward it."

"I know," Leon said, his eyes glued to what remained of the creature's profile strewn across the ground.

"Name's Greg. You?" Greg asked as he extended a bloody hand to Leon.

Leon extended his own and gave Greg a firm handshake. He glanced at the stain left on his palm and wiped the blood on his pant leg. "Le … Leroy," he stammered as he turned his face away, shifting his gaze to the corpse.

"Well, Leroy. You best be turning around and get yourself out of here as fast as you can, and as far away as you can. These bastards have spread out from the epicenter—damn prison. Can you believe that? How the hell does something like this happen, anyway?"

Leon ignored the question as he lowered his head and tugged the brim of his hat down a notch. "I have to find my fiancée."

"Fiancée, huh? Well, I guess that's as good a reason as any to walk toward the city center." Greg wasn't looking at Leon but instead faced away, scouring the area for movement. "Find her quick and then get out of here. The city is under lockdown. Most people are either dead or they have left. These things multiply faster than rabbits. When you're ready to leave, go back this way. It's one of the easier routes. The mall and the city's eastside are dismal. Still a lot of these things moving about, but the National Guard are working on it the best they can."

"Are you a part of the Guard?" Leon asked.

"Me? Shoot no. I'm just an old gun guy, looking for a fight," Greg chuckled. "These things make good target practice. But you gotta get 'em in the head. That's the only way they stay down. Women, or what they used to be, are hard to do, and I've run across a couple of kids. Sad, really, the little shits. They don't know what they are. Breaks my heart."

Leon noticed Greg's voice crack and grow softer as he spoke of the women and children. He swallowed hard.

"How bad is it by Pine and Coral?" Leon asked.

"Oh, that's fairly clear now. The cops had been in the area for a few days, clearing the looters and these creatures before the Guard showed up." Greg poked the body on the ground with the axe blade, then snatched a lengthy tree branch from the ground. He hacked the smaller twigs off, so he had a long branch that looked more like a walking stick. "You better take this with you. It's not much but it can keep them far enough away so you're not bitten. Aim for the head."

"Umm, thanks," Leon said as he reached for the stick.

"Find your girl and get out. Far away. These things are spreading out away from the prison at an exponential rate. The Guard isn't messing around either, so stay out of sight. 'Shoot first, check if you're human later' is their motto. If they can't contain this to the city, the whole country is fucked."

Leon's stomach tightened. His face still bent to hide his face, he gave a curt nod, not trusting his voice to speak. He held down the rush of bile threatening to burst from his insides.

He had to go to the lab. A cure, a reversal, something had to be done to fix what he alone had inflicted on their city.

How far had it spread?

Greg tipped his wide-brimmed sun hat and headed in the direction Leon had come from and yelled back, "Remember, don't let your guard down. Stay alert, stay alive."

Leon cleared his throat. "Umm—yeah. Got it. Thanks again."

A short distance later, while navigating through the deserted streets, Leon stumbled upon an abandoned book with an ornate cover, but no title. He picked it up and freed the side clasp. A diary. He scanned a few pages and sighed. It belonged to one of the prisoners. As he read more, his heart sank. The woman lamented over her sentence and days in prison. She was denied an appeal. Leon flipped through tear-stained pages, discovering the woman was wrongly accused and imprisoned for a crime she didn't commit. No one cared.

Did she turn into one of them, or did she run free? His mouth dropped open as the book slid from his hands. *Is that who I planted my heel into repeatedly a moment ago, bludgeoning her, or it, to death?*

His grandfather's voice snuck back into his head with a hint of sarcasm. "Son, she was already dead."

Hearing his grandfather's voice made him shudder.

What have I done?

Leon had to fix this nightmare he birthed into existence. The revelation fired Leon's soul. He had to do something—

find a cure. Get it out to everyone in the city. Reverse this madness. His determination raged on as he bent down and picked up the woman's diary and tucked it into his bag with care.

CHAPTER NINE

Leon reached the street corner near the laboratory building without encountering anyone. It was a miracle. He heard a jeep creep along the streets as he ducked into a doorway, letting the Guard personnel pass far out of sight before Leon resumed his journey. A glimpse of movement in the distance on two occasions, but he traveled in silence, not catching the attention of the undead as they shuffled along their meager existence.

Yet as he came up to the office building along the tree-lined side for cover, the graffiti scattered on the walkway and outside walls filled him with dread. What remained of a headless security guard nearby, it too was sprayed with paint. Leon stepped around the corpse and made a beeline toward the building then planted his feet, glaring ahead. Written in paint and marker, he saw what people thought of him.

"Rot in Hell."

"Die—sick bastard."

"Fleischer—coward."

"Prick!"

He stepped through the broken glass doors of the front entrance. A reporter must have posted the lab's address in their report. The company didn't advertise what they did in the building or list the address. The corporate office was the only location with publicly available contact information. This building was remote because of the controversial research they conducted. It stood at four stories, nothing ornate or eye-catching to distinguish the building from other similarly designed structures in the area. No company banner or sign was on the property to draw attention. It was an average gray brick building that blended into the city landscape.

The people believed Leon was responsible for plunging the city into madness. And they were right. That's what got under his skin. He'd destroyed an entire city with one calculated and malicious deed.

His shoulders sagged as he ascended six flights of stairs to his lab.

In the dwindling hours of daylight, amidst the hum of machinery and the flickering of fluorescent lights, Leon stared out the window. From the high vantage point, the streets looked like they had over the years, like nothing had disturbed the lives of every single human in Lindaire Hills. Yet he knew it was a façade, a charade. The world was a festering pile of muck and he'd thrown a bit of volatile fertilizer into the mix to make it explode. He smacked himself, just as his grandfather had smacked him as a young boy.

Leon vowed to correct his errors, promised himself to lead a quest for redemption. Perhaps not redemption, but at least a vaccine—a way to control the plague feeding on his city. His research notes and the rest of the serum were a place to start.

Had it spread beyond the city's borders? He had to know.

Science became not only a career but a vehicle for change, a way to rewrite the narrative of his family history. He sought to channel the pain, the guilt, and the complexity into a force for good. His thoughts drifted back to medical school. He had wanted to find a cure for his mother's illness. Not that it would bring her back, but he wanted to make her proud. As a child he'd been raised, scorned, and reshaped through praise and reprisal to seek his father's and grandfather's approval. But then and now, deep down, he wanted his mother to be proud of the man he'd become. He knew that was impossible now. Wherever her spirit was watching over him, he felt her celestial disappointment in his heart. He'd let her down.

Leon had become a monster, like his grandfather.

He mentally disconnected from himself, looking for objectivity, scouring his identity as if it were a specimen in one of the research cages or a sampling sliver under the intense scrutiny of a microscope. Or perhaps he needed to view himself as one of the reports would characterize him after such travesties.

Dr. Fleischer, the scientist, stood at the intersection of past and present, wrestling with his own demons while striving to shape a future untarnished by the shadows of his ancestry and his mistakes. Should the world forgive him and use his skills as a researcher to find a way to reverse the plague, or should they hold him accountable and let the undead feast on his living flesh?

The mental image of creatures tearing apart his flesh and feeding on his tender skin made Leon shudder.

He dumped out his medical bag and took inventory. In preparation for an emergency, he gathered the necessary essentials and left everything else behind. He'd go back to his apartment to work. He'd have food, water, and could feel relatively safe as long as no one knew he was there. The lab building was too big, too exposed to continue working there. He'd set out in the morning after sleeping on the all-too-familiar cot in his office.

A thump on his desk jolted Leon from the cot. He rubbed the sleep from his eyes, shielding the sunlight, and shook his head as his other hand reached for the long stick Greg had given him.

"What the fuck?"

"Dr. Leon, what are you doing here?" a young man asked with enthusiasm. He stood tall, a wisp of a man, hovering a bit out of reach of the stick pointed at him.

"Mick, is that you?"

"Yep, been here for two days. Today marks day three. The dorms kinda went to shit." Mick shrugged.

"Oh, I see," Leon said. "So no problems here?" He propped the stick back against the edge of the cot, then stretched, working out the stiffness from sleeping on the thin hard mattress.

"One came through the breakroom yesterday. He's smashed up between the wall and the refrigerator right now. I couldn't bring myself to kill it," Mick said with a sheepish smile. "I'm glad to see you're okay. All that business on the news. Crazy! You'd never do anything to hurt a fly much less cause this mess. Want some coffee?"

"Thanks, Mick. That'd be great." The joy Mick seemed to have for seeing Leon gave him comfort. Someone in the world was happy to see him.

"Sure thing, boss."

Mick trotted back with two steaming mugs and set them on Leon's desk. Leon grabbed a cup and wrapped his fingers around its warmth. He blew over the rim and then took a sip, letting the flavor and heat linger before swallowing.

"Anything left to eat in the breakroom?"

"Not much, I'm afraid. Some soup cans and stuff in the freezer. I've been avoiding the refrigerator after pinning Frankie there yesterday."

"Frankie?"

"Yeah, you know, after Dr. Frankenstein's monster. I had to give 'em a name."

Leon stared at the young man. Mick was nineteen, or was it twenty? Leon couldn't remember, but the boy was punctual, worked hard as an intern, and wanted to please everyone. Most of the staff were annoyed by his behavior, but Leon guessed the kid was hyperactive, undiagnosed. But the boy was smart, sociable, and did his job. Leon didn't mind Mick following him around most of the time. Recently, though, since Zoey had broken off their engagement, Leon had asked that Mick be reassigned to another scientist so he could have peace, labor through his thoughts, and work alone. They'd not talked in weeks.

"Frank is a fitting name," Leon said. "Let's see what we can find to eat."

After a filling breakfast of sausage and egg sandwiches and protein waffles, Leon felt energized. He even made a batch of orange juice from frozen concentrate.

As he drank his third cup of coffee, Leon chuckled watching Mick gobble up his fourth breakfast sandwich. "How do you eat so much and remain rail thin?" Leon asked.

"Genetics. My parents are still toothpick thin. Well, were, maybe?" Mick stopped for a moment and then shrugged. "I don't know how they're doing. I haven't been able to get a call through to let them know I'm okay." Mick chugged the last half of his orange juice, unfazed by the unknown state of his parents' lives.

"Do your parents live in the city?"

"No, they live in Wickerville, just over the river. There's been some buzz on the radio that a few of these crawler people have made it there and are causing a stir." Mick gestured toward Frankie with a tip of his crumb-laden chin.

"Doesn't that frighten you, that they could be hurt?"

"Well, gosh, Dr. Leon, of course. But my momma taught me not to fret about the unknown, especially if you can't do anything about it. This will sort itself out soon enough, and I'll get over to see them before returning to classes. I'm sure they're fine." Mick glanced at Frankie groaning and squirming while trapped by the angled refrigerator. "What do you suppose we should do with him?"

"I think we should move him so you can use whatever supplies are still edible. Then you should think about how to get to your parents. This isn't going to end anytime soon, and school is out of the question. The university isn't going to open back up for quite a while," Leon said. He stood and turned toward the door. "I'll be back in a minute. Coffee is running through me."

CHAPTER TEN

DUMB LUCK

When Leon returned to the breakroom, he saw through the glass window, Mick's fingers were going over the top of his phone—texting! He must have gotten through to his parents. Leon yanked his cell out of his back pocket and dialed Zoey. Nothing. So he tried a text and waited for the familiar 'undeliverable' notice to appear, but a ping happened instead. The message went through.

Leon turned away from the breakroom door and paced the hallway, back and forth, waiting for Zoey to reply. A line of dots appeared, then it stopped, so Leon stopped walking. Then another set of dots rolled across the screen. She was typing again, then that too stopped.

"Ugh, text me back! Let me know you're okay." Leon called out as he paced the floor again.

A minute or two passed, then his phone pinged again.

He stopped, blew out a breath, and pulled the screen up to read the message.

"We need to talk. I'm back in the city. Your place if you're still there. Tonight, 6pm."

Back in the city? Where had she gone?

Leon didn't care. He was focused on the fact that she texted him back and wanted to meet. His reply was immediate.

"Not there, but will be able to meet you tonight. At lab now."

Three dots moved along his screen then stopped. After a few seconds, he received a thumbs-up emoji, and nothing else. He waited for another message, but nothing came after the emoji. Disappointed, he replied, "Ok."

He walked, dragging his feet back toward the breakroom. It wasn't much, but she was alive. And she wanted to talk with him. The last thought gave him hope.

As Leon approached the breakroom door, he noticed Mick staring off to one side. As he swung the door open, Leon noted Frankie was not contained by the refrigerator. Instead, his stick lay on the floor and blood covered one end of the ragged branch.

"Mick? What happened, buddy?" Leon's eyes darted around the room, looking for Frankie as he cautiously stepped toward Mick.

Mick didn't answer.

Leon noticed the bottom of a boot near Mick's chair leg. The rest of the body was obscured by the table and chairs.

"Mick, talk to me."

Leon saw the blood seeping through Mick's shirt at the shoulder and sank into the seat beside the young man.

"Mom and Dad are good. Can't wait to see me," Mick said in a flat voice.

"How'd Frankie get out?"

"I was excited, not paying attention, and put the orange juice in the refrigerator. I slammed the door and sat down. Texted Mom again, and while I … oh boy. This isn't good, is it?" Mick's voice cracked.

"No, it's not," Leon said. He couldn't think of any words of comfort. Nothing could help the young man now.

"You're a doctor. Can't you stop it? Put a tourniquet on my shoulder and cut it off if you must," Mick said. Tears rolled down his cheeks. He let them fall.

Leon shook his head in reply. He rose and came around to Mick's side and pulled the blue button-up shirt aside to see how bad the bite was causing the bleed.

A perfect set of bite marks, each tooth hole full of blood, oozing across Mick's pale skin then grabbing the fabric of his shirt. Leon studied the surrounding skin. Already surface veins were dark and spreading like tiny worms crawling under Mick's skin.

Maybe I can save the boy if I act quickly. Tie the arm off and get him to a lab with surgical equipment. Just maybe.

He unbuckled his belt and pulled it off from around his waist. As he bent down and wrapped the leather under Mick's arm, he saw the dark trail crawl up the side of Mick's neck, the vein pulsing wildly as the darkness spread. There was no use, the virus was through the young man's system.

Leon threw his belt and watched it smack the door and fall to the tile floor with a thud.

"Guess that's a no, Dr. Leon?" Mick asked.

"I'm sorry, son. I can see the virus spreading through your veins." Leon gave Mick's other shoulder a slight squeeze and sat down across from the young man and looked him in the eye.

Mick let out a choked sob.

"If you leave now, maybe you can make it to see your parents before it takes over," Leon said. He knew the odds were slim, but it was all he could offer the boy.

"Nope. Can't do that to them. No one should have to watch their child turn into one of those—those things." Bitterness laced his words as Mick's head moved from side to side. "Nope, not going to do it."

Silence filled the room.

Leon looked at his phone. It was close to noon.

"Somewhere you gotta be, Dr. Leon?" Mick asked, his eyes blank.

"No, Mick. I'm here. Don't worry."

"Will you do me a favor? Well, two, actually. Answer two questions for me, honestly."

"Sure, whatever you need." Leon sat up, ready to help the poor lad.

"You didn't start all this madness, did you? The reporters got that wrong, didn't they?" Mick searched Leon's eyes as he asked the question.

Leon froze. His eyes held onto Mick's. He watched the transformation of Mick's face from innocent concern to realizing the truth, and then settling on disappointment.

Leon was familiar with disappointment.

"I did," Leon said. "I'm not going to lie to you, Mick. It's not going to help you."

"Why?" Mick asked.

"I knew I could do it. You know, be the one to solve our overpopulation problems. To help humanity, the earth, to raise us up, not tear us down." Leon sat up straighter.

"Like this? You envisioned this?" Mick pointed at Frankie while crunching up his face. "So, this is the result you were hoping for. Great job."

Leon noted Mick's dry sarcasm.

"Not this exactly. *This* was not on purpose, if that's what you're getting at. It was an experiment, the next stage of testing. But it resulted in a colossal fucking mistake, but it's done," Leon said flatly.

"Can you reverse it?" Mick failed to hide the hope in his voice. Then tossed another sarcastic jab at Leon. "Might as well make one more attempt at playing god. Am I right?"

"I don't know. I'm going to try. That's why I came here, to get the rest of the serum, the helicase enzyme, and study it. But now I'll take it home. I plan to reverse engineer it and find a way to control it, or a cure," Leon said.

Mick looked at Frankie's body decomposing on the floor at his feet. "Why take it home? You have everything you need here?"

"Not exactly. I noticed a couple pieces of equipment were destroyed. I have the older model of laser scanner at home. That should work well enough to read the DNA after separation. But I'll come back if needed for other equipment. Plus, it isn't safe here. It's too open."

Mick nodded, his eyes fixed on Frankie's face where he had jammed the tree branch through his mouth. "Yep, point proven. Okay, two more things, and you have to promise to do both."

"I said whatever you need."

"First, you have to do that to me." He extended an index finger to Frankie. "Don't let me turn into one of these monsters." Mick swung his head forward to meet Leon's gaze.

"Done. What else?" Leon asked.

"You were quick to agree, Dr. Leon," Mick said. His eyes turned to steel. His jaw clenched and released as he peered at Leon.

"I fought off a few of these on the way here, and I watched another man before that turn into one of these zombie-like creatures over a period of hours. It's the humane thing to do," Leon said. He shivered at the use of the word 'zombie.' He'd avoided thinking of these people, lifeless yet mobile, as an unrealistic character from a B-rated horror show. But it's what they were, zombies. And they were real.

"Fine." Mick's voice cut sharp. "After, let my parents know I won't be coming home." Mick's voice caught on the last words and he forced them out like a gravelly whisper.

"Least I can do," Leon said.

Leon glanced at the microwave's clock. He had six hours to make it home and see Zoey. Making this lad feel comfortable in his last hours was a gift. Leon could do that for the young man. He owed him that much—and more.

CHAPTER ELEVEN

DELIVERY

The look on Mick's face as Leon walked into the breakroom with a pistol and pulled the trigger haunted Leon more than he could fathom. Frightened, like a young deer frozen in headlights. Shocked still from the reality of death at his heels.

He'd almost forgotten about the pistol he'd stored in his office safe a few years ago. A colleague's spouse had come through security and shot up the place, upset about divorce papers and lost his mind. A guard had let the guy walk right through the front doors and into the elevator without having him go through the metal detectors. Leon went to the next gun show and bought a pistol to keep in the office. He didn't trust the guards anymore.

He mourned Mick. The boy was bright but had a simple charm, an innocence. Leon thought of the future Mick would never have, the research he'd never conduct for society's betterment. He'd been Leon's protégé for a time. The career he'd taken from Mick and countless others as they'd turned into these ravenous beasts over the past several days ate at him. Leon gagged on bile rising from his churning stomach.

Leon knew it was the kindest way to end the young man's suffering. But Mick had opened his mouth. Leon considered stopping for a fraction of a second. The thought flew away as quickly as it had arrived. He strode forward and pulled the trigger anyway. Mick's gasp, or whatever he was about to say or do ensured Leon didn't have to pull the trigger a second time. For that he was thankful, yet Leon's heart broke for the lad. He couldn't deal with contacting Mick's parents right away. He'd contact them later.

Leon was two blocks from his apartment when he came upon an older woman leaning against a building. Her head was down and she was mumbling to herself. He slowed his pace and maneuvered himself out of reach as he approached in case she was infected by his plague.

She looked up with weariness in her eyes. Her gaze landed on his medical bag and she perked up. "Help me, please. You are a doctor, no?" she asked, her accent thick.

Leon pushed past the woman.

"My daughter, please help us. She is in labor. I think the baby needs to turn more," she said. Her hand grabbed onto his arm.

He stopped and glanced at her hand clinging to him before stepping back and twisting away.

She pulled her arm close and raised both hands in the air. "I'm sorry. I'm sorry. We're all alone. She cannot travel due to—this." The woman waved her arms wildly around as she choked on a sob.

"I'm not a medical doctor, ma'am," Leon said.

"But you know how to turn a baby, no?"

He thought for a moment about his medical training long ago. "Yes, but it is a risky procedure. Are you saying the baby has not turned, but she's in labor?" Leon asked.

"Yes, she's been in labor for hours now, but the baby's head is still up here." The woman tapped herself just under her breasts. "I cannot move it enough. I'm afraid the feet will move down soon."

He learned in medical school how to handle breech deliveries, but he was a researcher now. He hadn't ever delivered a baby.

"I'd like to help but that's not my specialty. I'm a researcher. Maybe fifty percent of doctors are successful in turning a breech and keeping it facedown for delivery."

"That does not matter. This baby comes now." The woman pointed her finger to the ground and stomped a foot. "Either we try to move the baby, or …or I might lose them both."

Leon pulled the brim of his cap down and shook his head. If the woman wasn't ready to deliver, he might miss meeting Zoey. "I am meeting my fiancée in a bit. Are you sure she'll deliver soon?"

He was responsible for so much destruction. Could he really leave this family to struggle to deliver a breech baby on their own? They could potentially kill two innocent people. Could he live with himself if he did nothing and walked away?

Help the woman.

He felt the universe give him a gentle nudge. Maybe his mother's spirit was near. He didn't know. What felt certain was that if he didn't assist, this would also fester and torment him. He had to see something good happen. Something he could feel he did right while the world crumbled around him, reminding him constantly that he had caused all this chaos and misery.

"Okay. Where are we going?"

Leon crouched over a coffee table in the corner of the small apartment's living room swaddling a newborn. He and June, the little boy's grandmother, had worked as a team to turn and position the little guy for delivery. It seemed as soon as he was maneuvered with his head down, the little tyke knew what to do and his mother's labor, although suddenly more intense, was productive. Glenmore Ireneo arrived in minutes.

Leon counted ten perfect fingers and ten perfect toes. He marveled at the ability to build a human being from nothing more than a few cells. Every creature on earth, the females of the species were miracle workers. From all accounts, Glenmore would be a healthy baby. Leon passed the bundled boy to his mother, who was eager to hold her son.

Leon had only been able to build something that was destroying the world outside these walls. An abomination. A shiver ran down his back.

"The bathroom?" Leon asked. "So I can clean up."

The young mother pointed down the narrow hall to their right without taking her eyes off the boy.

Ten minutes later, Leon returned to the kitchen for a glass of water and found June reading from a binder.

His binder.

"Ma'am, please. Close tha—"

"Shush," June said. She held out her hand to stop him. "Do not say a word."

Leon slunk into a nearby chair, the metal legs grating across the tile floor as he sat. He knew she'd discovered who he was and what he'd done. Nothing he said or did would change that fact. He held his head in his hands, elbows resting on the small dinette table, and waited for June to speak.

Would she understand? He was a changed man, changed and touched by the miracle of life in this very apartment. The creation June's daughter had grown and nourished inside of herself, it was a blessing he'd not pondered from a mother's perspective. How insignificant he felt. His aspirations pure folly.

He was reminded of something his father had said about his mother after Leon had caught them yelling one day. His father had said, "If you give a woman something, she will make something much more useful, or troublesome for you, depending on what you gave or did to her. If you purchase a house, she will fill it with beautiful furnishings, prepare delicious meals, and make that purchase into a warm and loving home. If you make trouble in some way, a woman will multiply that and it will backfire onto you, making life more difficult. Remember son, what you give a woman multiplies. Be prepared for the consequences."

His father had laughed after, but Leon sensed there was a deeper meaning, a hurt his father had caused his mother that could not be undone.

Leon understood. He'd caused great harm that had multiplied a hundredfold and could not be undone. The death. The destruction. He couldn't undo any of it. Even a cure could not undo the damage already done.

A creeping thought that had lingered at the periphery of his mind over the past several days reared up, showing itself in all its sinister light. He couldn't push it away.

The world is better off without you.

A shudder escaped his lips. Although he knew he deserved such thoughts and to take such action, he couldn't do it. He had work to do. Leon had to find a cure and get it out to the world quickly. He breathed in a long, slow breath and raised his head.

Smack!

Leon's eyes watered from the force of the blow.

June stood over him, shaking. A towering spectacle of maternal understanding and protective instincts, June's energy was a force to be reckoned with—an unseen power Leon sensed was full of ancient wisdom. She glowered at him with such hatred, Leon could feel it seeping from her stare. Leon cowered.

He touched his cheek—the same way he'd cupped it as a child after one of his grandfather's brutal slaps. But this smack was different. He deserved it, and so much more for the evil he'd unleashed into the world.

He nodded his head as she cursed and spoke in her Creole tongue. June brandished him with a slew of retorts for using things he did not understand. Leon caught a word here and there he understood 'jimson weed' from the ingredients noted in the binder, and then June said 'curse' a while later. She whispered her vehement tongue lashing and would look around the corner at her daughter and grandson from time to time. When June stopped to catch her breath, Leon opened his mouth to speak, but she quickly waved a hand in his face and clamped her fingers together as if to yell "Shut up!"

Leon sat back and waited for her to start again.

"You do not practice things you don't understand," she said, folding her arms while continuing to glare at Leon. "Intentions fuel such a vile curse."

She stood silent for a few more minutes before simply saying, "You are evil man. You bring evil." She paused and bit her lip, then waved a finger in his face. "I know who you are, Dr. Fleischer. You helped my daughter, so I will not call police. Not yet."

Leon shrugged and nodded, defeated by her flat tone. She was not wrong. He was evil.

The front door creaked as it slowly opened, and a young man entered the cramped apartment. He looked around anxiously before catching sight of June. He slid the door closed behind him without a sound.

The man stepped over to June and they spoke in a hushed tone before he left to go by her daughter's side.

"My son-in-law. Do not speak," June said and went to leave Leon alone in the kitchen, then stopped. She glared over her shoulder and hissed, "Do not speak."

Leon did as he was told and remained quiet. He could hear June whispering and the man interjecting intermittently. As he waited, Leon tip-toed to his medical bag and placed the binder inside slowly so as to not make noise.

The energy in the air shifted as the seconds ticked loudly from the wall clock.

Leon sensed he was no longer welcome. No, knew he was no longer welcome. He gathered his belongings and slipped on his jacket without a word. Their eyes bore into him as he made his way with silent steps toward the door. He stepped through the entryway, closed the apartment door gently behind him, and then shook, releasing the pent-up anxiety he'd felt since June read his research notes.

Yes, you are an evil man. Runs in the family. Embrace it.

His grandfather's voice again.

"Shut up!" Leon yelled into the empty hallway.

CHAPTER TWELVE

DAMNATION

Leon left June and her family without pleading for their understanding or forgiveness. He knew their future, and the future of her new grandson was in peril. Assisting in the birth may have given him a slight reprieve, but it was not enough to cleanse him of his burden and the guilt he felt for the evil he'd brought to their doorstep.

He stepped into the afternoon sun and let its warmth flow over his face. He had an hour and a half until Zoey was to arrive. His apartment was only a few blocks north, and he realized he was excited to see Zoey after so long a time since they last saw each other. It'd been at least two months. Had it been longer? Time felt as if it had slipped through his fingers. Working alone in the lab for so long and then the nightmarish reality surrounding him made him lose all sense of time.

The absurdity of people turning into these creatures, creatures he was responsible for creating, felt so unreal, incomprehensible.

The cell phone vibrated in his jacket pocket. His face wrinkled not remembering he set the phone to vibrate. When he pulled the phone out, Leon realized it was Mick's phone. His parents had texted a dozen times while Leon had delivered the child upstairs.

Leon took a long, deep breath and blew it out. Might as well get this over with. He sent a brief message.

"This is not Mick. I have news."

"What? Who is this? Where is our son?"

Leon shook his head. *Just get it over with, there's no easy way. Just tell them.*

"I have bad news. Mick is gone."

. . .

. . .

"No. You're lying. He was coming home. He told us so."

"I'm sorry. He was attacked at the office. He's gone," Leon typed out.

"Who is this? How do you know?"

"Leon."

"You're the man on the news! Did you hurt Mick?"

"No. Well, yes," Leon said, flustered. "There's nothing more to say. I'm sorry."

Leon glared at the phone as Mick's mother was still typing. Nothing he said would bring their son back. Leon bowed his head and slowly crept to a trashcan. He tossed Mick's phone into it as another message popped up on the screen.

"You are evil! What did you do to our son?"

Tell me something I don't know.

Leon was a hundred yards from his apartment building when sounds pulled his mind from daydreaming of Zoey. He heard shuffles and thumps from behind. He whirled around and saw a group of the undead were on his heels. Soon surrounded, Leon pushed and jabbed his long stick at one after the other of the creatures, trying to keep them at bay.

One pulled at his backpack, throwing him off balance. He wrestled to regain his footing but faltered. The gurgling noises from their throats, along with odd howls of excitement or pain Leon could not discern, but the noises unnerved him.

Sweat dripped from his brow and his hands were damp. His grip on the wooden weapon slipped and he crashed to the ground. The undead clawed at his shirt. He slipped out of the backpack and dragged his medical bag on the ground as he grappled to push through the horde on his hands and knees.

A long blade flew to his right, and a body flopped to the ground next to him, spraying Leon's eyes and open mouth with blood. Leon spat and panted as he rushed to clear himself from a set of gnashing teeth.

A voice shouted above the throng of undead. "Get out! We got this, just clear out of the way."

Leon rushed toward the voice, his hands slapping the pavement with each advance. The blacktop cut into his hands as he worked to find an exit. He turned left and another creature dropped in front of his face. A blade had cut through the thing's head and blood spread, dark and velvety, across the road. Leon slapped his hands through the creature's blood, and his knees ground into the soppy mess as he charged for a clearing. As he stood, the sun basked him in warmth. Yet the stench of rotting iron and sweet decomposition filled the air.

He retreated from the crowd, observing two people battling the horde. Leon witnessed swords and makeshift pokers dwindle the thrashing undead down to a motionless stack of bodies. When all was quiet, one of the attackers walked around stabbing skulls; the other walked to Leon.

"You okay, man?" a man with a thick beard and long ponytail asked.

"Yeah-yeah, I think so," Leon said.

"How did they get so close to you? Didn't you hear them coming up on you? By the way, name's Jack." Jack motioned to the other person still jabbing skulls. "That's Katie. She's a little skittish about these things getting back on their feet. If you know what I mean.

"Yeah, I can understand that. Thanks for the help," Leon said, still rattled from scrambling for his life. "My head wasn't in the game. Daydreaming, I guess."

Jack moved away and touched Katie on the shoulder. "All right, guy. Glad we were walking through and you're all right. We're getting out of here before it gets dark. Suggest you do the same."

"Thanks again. I'm right here." Leon waved a finger toward his apartment complex.

"Good. Get cleaned up. You look like shit."

The rest of the way to his apartment was uneventful. He had 45 minutes before Zoey's arrival, sufficient time for a shower and a drink. Not necessarily in that order.

CHAPTER THIRTEEN

HOME

As Leon cleared the entrance of the building his emotions flooded over. He rushed into a working elevator and tapped the buttons until the doors closed, impatient to get into his familiar surroundings. The elevator chimed, reaching the eighth floor. He hurried down the hall to his apartment.

Once inside, Leon worked the locks on his door, turned and leaned against it. Feverish with energy, he pulled a desk and chair in front of the door to block anyone from entering. He wanted a shower in peace.

Breathing heavily, he closed his eyes, brainstorming for a solution to the destruction. Moments crept by, his breathing calmed but he kept his eyes closed.

A vision of him and his mother kneeling in prayer when he was a small boy, flew across his mind.

Leon fell to his knees. He clasped his hands together tightly like he used to and spoke in a whisper.

"Dear Lord, what have I done? I know it is unforgivable. In my exhaustion and arrogance, I twisted a tale of lies in my mind to support my ignorance. Please forgive my stupidity.

Help me to stop the evil from spreading. I am to blame. If you see fit to punish me, so be it. But guide me now to do the right thing."

Ten minutes passed, yet Leon knelt in silence in his blood-drenched pants, the crimson fluid seeping into the carpet. His fingers and palms stung. The guilt and self-loathing overwhelmed him as the weight of the situation pressed on his mind. A tear dripped from his cheek and splattered on the floor.

How can Zoey love me after she realizes I'm to blame for everything?

Exhausted and achy, Leon pulled himself from the floor and sat in the chair. Quietly he picked up the landline phone and dialed Zoey's number, then waited. After several rings, the call made it through. Zoey answered.

"Zoey, please don't hang up."

"Leon? You sound awful. I'm on my way but will be late. Maybe closer to seven—travel isn't easy anymore."

"Zoey, just listen. I understand. Don't hang up until you hear me out, please." Leon felt the pleading in his voice but he didn't care.

"You have one minute," Zoey said, her tone guarded.

"I've been thinking. Zoey, with everything that's happened lately. Don't you understand? I want a future with you, away from my work, from all of this—a fresh start. I love you. If that means I must leave my project, that's okay. You're more important than any of that. Let's start fresh somewhere else. What do you say?"

Zoey couldn't believe what she heard. "Really? And what about kids?"

The lack of emotion in her voice wasn't lost on Leon, but he pressed further. "Whatever you want, Zoey. We'll have as many children as we can manage. Did I tell you I delivered a baby today? A precious little boy. It was a miracle in this madness. I've realized my mistakes and want to start over if I'm able."

"You have no idea how happy that makes me, to hear you say that, Leon!"

He could hear the change to her voice. She was almost jovial in her response. Relief swept over him as he realized she may forgive him. They could be together again.

"Leon, there's something I need to tell you, too." She was quiet for a moment before continuing. "But I want to tell you in person. I'll be there soon."

Silence.

"Leon? You there?"

"Yes, darling, I'm here," he said. His voice trembled, knowing he had to tell her the truth if they were to have a real future together. He couldn't hide the research he needed to do to find a cure. "I have something to tell you, too."

"I'll see you soon."

The line clicked off. Leon stared at the receiver.

Refreshed after a shower and a double scotch, Leon stood over the kitchen counter, laboring over the notes and photos he'd spread out.

June's harsh comments came flooding back to him. He scribbled a few words on the side of a notebook page—

voodoo, intent, curse. Was there more to the serum than the ingredients? Did he call upon an unknown force summoning a curse? Leon wasn't certain, but he felt he was on to something and wrote vigorously in his notebook. The forcefulness of the pen in his fingertips made his hand ache. He put the pen down and rubbed his hands together. The more he rubbed the more they hurt. Just as he turned a palm over to look at it, the doorbell rang.

Leon ran to the door and shoved the table and chair away and opened the door.

Zoey took a hesitant look at Leon and walked past him into the apartment. She wore a heavy oversized tunic with leggings and utility boots. She had a shotgun over her shoulder. Everything about her attire was unusual for Zoey and took Leon by surprise.

Leon watched her walk in. She placed the shotgun against the couch, stepped into the kitchen and turn to face him. She appeared the same even though he hadn't seen her in months. Her hair was a little longer, and ruffled, not sleek like he'd grown accustomed to seeing her wear it.

"You look terrible, Leon. Are you okay?" Zoey took a step to close the gap between them, then stopped. Her eyes shifted to the pile of papers on the counter. "What is all this?"

"Don't!" Leon jumped. "Let me explain first." He positioned himself between Zoey and the counter full of papers.

"I thought you said you were done with your research?" Zoey asked. Stepping back from Leon, anger clipped her words.

"I said I was done with the project. *That project*. This is something different and what I wanted to talk with you about, among other things." Leon let the last few words trail to a whisper.

"Well, that's one reason why we broke up—your work. I couldn't talk about it then. I was so angry, and I knew you'd try to convince me to go through with the wedding. I don't want a wedding. I don't want you involved in this." She grabbed a handful of paper and tossed it across the counter. "And I knew I have no right to tell you what to do, so I ran to take a break. To let my head clear. Your research with the serum devastated me. It goes against everything I believe in."

"There's something fundamentally wrong with that project. Everything about it shouted evil. It was like you were playing God. Choosing who lived and who died at your fingertips. And now, look what you've done. This city, these zombies, they're everywhere. You played God and failed at everyone's expense." Zoey shook with anger, her hands curled into tight fists.

Heat crawled up Leon's face. His eyes clouded as Zoey let her feelings pour out.

"And it's not up to you to dictate how the world deals with overpopulation. It sounded so crazy to me. Using this project, this control method thing of yours." Zoey waved her hand toward the sprawling mess of papers. "Women decide, not you. This isn't the dark ages. Men think they can control everything, and it's never been the case. Women nurture and grow a human being. Without women controlling their destiny, the world becomes nothing but chaos."

Tears fell over and down Leon's face as he listened and realized he had destroyed a beautiful future in a matter of a few days. She would never forgive him once she knew the truth.

"Why are you crying?" She crossed her arms then quickly dropped them to her sides.

"You're right, that's all." His voice was full of defeat and despair. "Zoey, this is my fault. All of it. The plague ravaging the city, it is my doing. Don't you understand? You need to go, get out of the city as quickly as you can."

"I was out of the city. I came back to see you—one last time. I had to speak my mind before I left for good," Zoey said.

Leon understood. There'd be no reconciliation. No life with this woman who could help him be a better man. "Go to your mom's house. If I can get there—I'll try. I must find a way to fix this mess. But promise me you will go now. Take care of yourself. I love you."

Zoey's mouth hung open. She didn't believe what she was hearing. Leon sounded lost—resigned.

"Leon! Leon, what do you mean? What more have you done? Don't you have an anti-venom or vaccine or something?" Her voice cracked on the last word.

"It's no use, Zoey. I can't explain it now. I realize it's too much for anyone to forgive. Just go, please. Pack and leave now." Leon was flustered. He looked at the palms of his hands and gasped.

There were muffled grunts and banging coming from outside the apartment. They turned toward the commotion, dropping their conversation.

Leon noticed the locks unlatched. He'd forgotten to reset them after Zoey walked in.

"Go to the bathroom. Lock yourself in and don't come out until I check on you."

"Leon. It's probably a neigh—"

"Go!" Leon said as he glanced down. His hands were black and swollen. Veins pulsed dark up his wrists as if fighting for oxygen.

Leon heard the bathroom door lock as the front door cracked, the weight of the horde causing it to splinter and heave. He rushed to latch the locks as the door gave way causing his leg to get pinned by the door's edge. Leon counted as the undead climbed over each other to get into the apartment. His apartment.

Once the pressure was off the door, he was able to scramble to a standing position. The undead shuffled about as if in a daze. Why didn't they attack him?

Leon grabbed the long walking stick and cautiously stepped closer to the nearest creature. It peered at him as if confused. Leon poked it, nudging it and piercing the skin.

The creature responded by sniffing the air and grunting. It pressed toward him, jutting its head about as if blind.

Leon looked at the others. A series of sounds—cries, clicks, and groans shared in a disorienting cacophony that irked him. The nearest one shuffled, head jerking, as if deciding what to do.

Movement from the others caught his attention. One was advancing toward the back of the apartment, toward the bathroom. Toward Zoey.

Leon slammed the stick into one creature nearest to him and it belted out a horrifying wail. The others stopped in their tracks and moved as a united front toward Leon. The fear of one of them getting to Zoey sent his mind spiraling. He had to defeat these things—all of them.

He grabbed Zoey's shotgun, cocked it, and blew a hole through one creature's skill. He tried again. Click. Empty. He tossed the weapon and picked up a glass lamp, throwing it across their route. The glass smashed across the floor, leaving a path of shards.

Grabbing a kitchen knife from the counter, Leon jumped into the group of the undead. He pushed and swung his arm, slicing at anything in his orbit. One fell onto the coffee table, crashing to the floor, wood and glass flying in all directions.

Again one of the creatures ventured toward the back of the apartment.

Leon screamed, "Come get me!" as he launched himself at what should have been a woman in the prime of her life. He swiped the blade across the back of her head. Blood oozed like a rushing creek down her back.

Even then his scientific mind was working. He knew the blood was no longer pumping through their veins. In all aspects, only the primitive synapses of the mind remained, persisting against all odds. Like death rattles that refused to stop. It disgusted him that he'd created these monsters. That he was their creator.

He pulled his arm back and brought it forward, severing the dead woman's head. Leon watched as it hit the wall and bounced to the ground. Dark crimson, almost black, stained the floor in a radiating puddle.

Another clamored to get past Leon and the headless corpse. A man this time. Leon had to keep reminding himself that these were no longer people. Mindless shells driven by survival instincts. They were simply electrodes pulsating from the weakest part of the brain, an instinctual need to survive no matter how or why.

Leon wrestled with the creature, shoving it to and fro as he inched them in unison toward the stick, knocking into shelves and the other two creatures as they scuffled. He reached for the weapon, his comfortable companion as he'd strode through the streets to get home, and wrapped his swollen hand around the familiar wooden staff. With one solid motion, he thrust the spear up through the jaw and into the creature's skull.

It gurgled in response and fell to the floor, the walking stick tightly held into place, its hands and legs jerking with the same repetitive motion Leon had witnessed of the office clerk's brain matter.

It was all science.

Leon made quick measure of another as he tussled toward his medical bag. He still had the pistol from his office in the bottom of the bag. If only he could get close enough to find it, he could dispense with the remaining horde and barricade the door long enough to map a route of escape for Zoey.

With one hand, he kept the old man at bay while rummaging through his bag for the revolver. Leon found the cool metal and slid his finger into the trigger guard. He pulled the weapon out. In one quick motion, Leon jammed the barrel into the old man's mouth and pulled the trigger.

He'd had enough. Weakened and wondering why it was quiet, Leon turned toward where he thought the remaining creature had been. It was gone.

Frantic, Leon rushed toward the bedroom and found two men struggling on his bed. He backed away and covered the bathroom door. Zoey had to be inside, unharmed.

"Zoey, stay put," he said over the commotion.

"What's going on?" she asked.

"Stay there."

With a thud and crash, the bed frame gave way, sending the two men tumbling to the floor. Leon realized one no longer had his head as it rolled across his feet, trailing a semi-circle of blackish drippings as it rolled along.

The other man stood and straightened his shirt in a huff.

"Ray?" Leon asked.

"Yeah. What happened to you?" Ray replied.

Leon ignored him and rushed back to the front door, sliding the desk over the open doorway.

Ray followed him.

Leon stacked anything of size on top of the desk, while Ray rinsed off his hands in the kitchen sink.

"Don't do that yet. I gotta get Carla. She's hiding in a room a few doors down." Ray slid items aside and climbed over the desk. He stood in the hallway, looking back at Leon. Ray peered at Leon's hands and his exposed skin, dark and veiny. "You don't look good."

Trembling and horrified, Zoey cried, tears brimmed over and cascaded down her face. Trying to understand, she couldn't comprehend what she was hearing … until silence.

And more silence.

Leon didn't return to get her.

After several minutes, she pressed an ear against the door and breathily asked, "Leon? Leon, are you all right? I'm coming out now."

CHAPTER FOURTEEN

SENTENCE

Zoey twisted the door handle so as not to make a sound. Every corner of the apartment was in shambles. The bed was broken, and a decapitated man lay bloodied and mangled. She took one hesitant step and then another until she stood in the opening of the narrow hallway.

Everything was destroyed in the living room. Glass, wood, metal was scattered among blood and death. The smell made her sick, and she threw up in the trashcan. Only the desk, pulled against the open doorway, remained unbroken.

She stepped into the living room and turned toward the adjacent wall. Leon sat sprawled out on his chair. Already a stench of rot simmered in the air. There was blood everywhere, from floor to ceiling, with pieces of flesh clinging to the walls. Her eyes couldn't withdraw from Leon for long. So she allowed herself to gaze at him. Blood had seeped from open wounds across his chest, arms, and neck, pooling at his waist from the recent onslaught. His face, hung down, slightly turned toward the door, greeting her with a wretched gaze of death.

His dangling arm hung over the armrest with black and swollen fingers. Oozing sores dripped deep black blood like motor oil dripping from a leaky gasket.

Leon held the rotary phone receiver in his other hand, now covered in blood and pieces of torn flesh. Faintly she heard the recorded message "Please hang up the phone and try your call again."

Slowly she walked forward, trembling, hands to her mouth, unable to fathom the scene. She fell to her knees as she reached Leon. Sobbing, she sat in shock and rested her head on his knees, continuing to weep.

Leon's arm twitched with a slight, almost undistinguishable, movement. Yet it was enough that he dropped the telephone receiver.

Zoey's sobs grew silent. Holding her breath, she opened her eyes while still resting her head on his lap. Unsure of what made the sudden noise, she listened and waited ...

Slowly, Leon's head shifted, turning toward Zoey at his feet. A deep, guttural rumble came from his chest as his fingers dug into Zoey's forearm.

"Ouch! Leon, you're hurting me!" she cried. Zoey heard heavy footsteps from the hallway, drawing her attention from what was once her fiancé.

Was that help coming, or another of the undead?

Bile rose in her throat as her gaze shifted back to Leon as his grip tightened. "Let go! Le—"

A shot assaulted her ears. Horrified, her eyes bulged as she stared where Leon's face should have been. Blood splatter littered her cheeks, hair, and shoulders.

Dazed, her eyes traveled the bullet's trajectory to brain matter and bone fragments covering the wall.

"Miss? Miss, are you all right?" Ray scrambled over the desk and rushed to Zoey, pulling her away from Leon into the kitchen where there was less mess. "Wait here."

Ray ran over to the entry and pulled Carla into the apartment.

Carla rushed to Zoey's side. "You must be Zoey. I'm Carla, this is my husband, Ray."

"How-how do you know my name?" Zoey asked, her hands shaking as she reached for a glass.

"Leon told us about you. We met after all of this started. He helped Ray and me get back to the city to find our family. Unfortunately, we were too late." Carla glanced at Ray. "He gave us this address in case we needed a place to stay."

Zoey eyed Ray as she gulped a glass of water. "You shot Leon."

"He wasn't Leon anymore," Ray said flatly. "I could tell he'd turn when I saw him fighting the undead. Look at his hands and veins. He was infected."

Zoey nodded. She saw the dark gray haze under Leon's skin and how his blood oozed out thick and dark. She shuddered and started to wipe the tears from her face.

Carla stopped her bloody hand and pulled it down. "Don't get anything near an open wound or your mouth." She then pulled a kitchen towel out of a drawer and ran it under water until it was warm. Carla helped Zoey clean the blood and muck from her hands. She inspected her, as Leon had Carla and Ray inspect each other at the store.

Even as Zoey trembled, her stomach growled.

Carla's stomach rumbled in reply. "We need to eat," Carla said.

Zoey looked at Carla's bump in her tummy and ran her hand across her own stomach. "Yes, we do."

Each of the women let out an anxious chuckle.

Ray watched in amazement as the two women rummaged through the refrigerator and cupboards for food as the dead lay scattered, the stench of rot and decay growing with each tick of the clock. He joined the women and they ate as they each picked up the papers and notes Leon had left scattered across the countertop.

"What do you think this is?" Carla asked. She took a napkin and wrapped her fingers around something in Leon's medical bag and brought out a small vial of purple liquid.

"That is what started all of this," Zoey said with confidence. "His serum to control population, to terminate women's pregnancies." She touched her growing stomach as she finished the last sentence.

Carla and Ray locked eyes. Carla put the vial back into the bag.

Ray asked, "Did he know you were pregnant?"

"No. I never told him," Zoey said, shaking her head side to side. "Actually, it's better this way. I knew it couldn't work out between us. I came here tonight to tell him about the baby and make a clean break."

"Ahhhh," Carla said as her eyes glanced around.

Looking at the destruction and death in the small apartment, Zoey shrugged. "Mission accomplished?"

"Let's get out of here," Ray said. "There's a National Guard checkpoint set up nearby. We can drop the vial with the CDC rep there, along with his notes. Someone else can figure out this mess. You two ladies have been through enough. Those babies need a safe place to grow up and it isn't in this city."

Zoey nodded. "I couldn't agree more." She stood, walked over to Leon's body and scoured every aspect of the scene, committing it to memory. "Sometimes this is how he seemed internally—diseased and broken—a wickedness seeping out of his pores. No matter how much I had hoped he was redeemable, I think my heart knew all along it was impossible. It's a shame he could never escape his own demons."

Carla gently touched Zoey on the shoulder. "Let's go."

Without looking back, Zoey followed her new companions out the door.

EPILOGUE

A decade later.

Zoey crouched between rows of beans, breaking them off the plants and placing the fresh vegetables into a basket. Isack, her son, stood by grape vines a few yards away, inspecting the small green clusters for signs of ripening. A man, tall and lean, came hobbling out of the woods toward them.

Zoey stood and told Isack to fetch his aunt from the house. He did as his mother asked.

The man continued to walk toward Zoey with a limp. He stopped and glanced over his shoulder as if listening for something. When he turned back, his eyes were tearing and full of dread.

Zoey stood tall. Her hand rested at the small of her back where she kept a compact Glock 19 in her waistband.

Isack pushed through the front door with Ella, Carla, and Ray following. All four stood side-by-side with weapons drawn on the front porch. Isack with a bow aimed at the man's chest. Carla's and Ray's son, Charlie, peered around the door frame with the other children skirting his flank.

As the man approached within thirty feet of Zoey, she waved him off. "Stop. What do you want?"

"Want? Nothing, ma'am. I've been stopping by homes along the Appalachian Trail as I hike through to share a desperate message."

Zoey peered at him cautiously, taking in the ragged clothing and battered gear on his back. "What's the message?" Zoey asked.

"It's no longer contained," he said.

"What's not contained?" As the words left her mouth, Zoey knew what he meant.

THE END

ACKNOWLEDGEMENTS

I wouldn't be able to do what I love without the encouragement and support of my husband, Steve, and grown children, Stephen and Elena. Thank you for tolerating the crazy discussions from scientific principles, character analysis of racist jerks, to all the other mutterings that went into crafting this tale. It was a ride.

A huge thanks to my beta readers: Elena, Chris, and Steve. Thank you for your thorough comments, generous swipes of your bleeding pens, and for your invaluable input and inspiration.

Genie, you are a blessing. I appreciate your availability and editing expertise to help bring this story to fruition on a tight deadline.

ABOUT THE AUTHOR

Sirrah Medeiros served years ago in the U.S. Marine Corps, trained as a Marine Water Dog. The experiences in water purification inspired her toward environmental studies, and she later graduated from the University of Maryland with honors in Environmental Management. After many career changes from logistics, teaching, owning a few businesses, to defense contracting, Sirrah retired from defense work as a program manager in 2020. She now pursues her creative passions as a writer and editor of dark fiction, and she will pick up an art pencil to draw from time to time. For a full list of her published work, visit her website, www.sirrahmedeiros.com. Sirrah lives in Virginia with her family and two rescue dogs.

ALSO BY THE AUTHOR

The Emerald Curse
Secrets of Mother

9 798985 202540